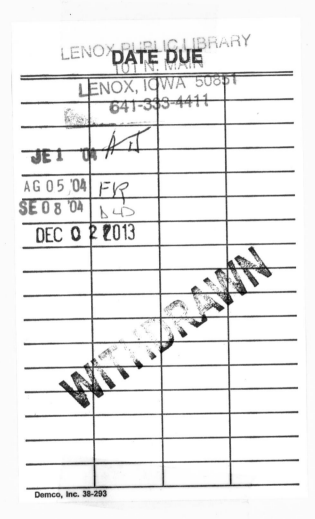

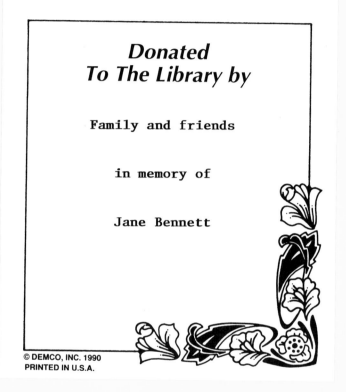

Donated
To The Library by

Family and friends

in memory of

Jane Bennett

Gunsmoke Empire

**Center Point
Large Print**

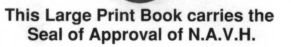

**This Large Print Book carries the
Seal of Approval of N.A.V.H.**

ॐ श्री गणेशाय नमः

Gunsmoke Empire

Lewis B. Patten

Center Point Publishing
Thorndike, Maine

This Center Point Large Print edition
is published in the year 2002 by arrangement with
Golden West Literary Agency.

The text of this Large Print edition is unabridged. In other
aspects, this book may vary from the original edition. Printed in
Thailand. Set in 16-point Times New Roman type by
Bill Coskrey and Gary Socquet.

ISBN 1-58547-214-X

Library of Congress Cataloging-in-Publication Data.

Patten, Lewis B.
    Gunsmoke empire / Lewis B. Patten.--Center Point large print ed.
        p. cm.
    ISBN 1-58547-214-X (lib. bdg. : alk. paper)
    1. Large type books. I. Title.

PS3566.A79 G87 2002
813'.54--dc21
                                                            2002019138

Chapter One

MEMORY IS A STRANGE THING, like a gusty wind, blowing strong against me at times, at others weakening until it is only a gentle breeze. For instance, I scarcely remember the war years, except for a few scattered recollections—high points like the booming of cannon in the distance, and once the plain crackle of musket fire in the woods near our house.

I suppose I remember the smells best of all, and to this day I never get the acrid bite of powdersmoke in my nostrils but what the feel of that time and place comes back, drifting over me like the blue cloud of musket smoke that drifted out of the woods that day.

Different sounds stir different memories. The baying of a hound can make me shiver yet. Hearing it, and shivering, I'll remember my mother's harried but still beautiful face as plain as anything.

I remember other small things—being hungry often, and cold sometimes. There was never enough of anything—never quite enough.

And the hiding place under the porch where she always sent me when someone was coming. No, not just someone—only the Yankees. Why she thought they'd hurt a small boy, I don't know, but there were a lot of ugly stories floating around the country then and she probably believed them.

She wasn't so much afraid of regular Yankee troops, but she lived in deathly fear of those renegade raiders who masked their activities under the Union flag. And the deserters, from whom no woman was ever safe.

The wind is gusty now, blowing strong with the unbelievable terror of that night, but shock has rendered the memory unreal, as though it happened to someone else instead of to me.

We heard the hound bay first. Then we heard a shot, and the hound was silent. Mother sent me down under the back porch, and a few minutes later I heard the approaching sound of men's voices.

If Mother had had a gun in the house, things might have been different. But the Confederacy's guns were at the front with the fighting men.

Mother and I had just finished carrying our supper of greens, cooked with a shank of ham, from the cabin out in the yard which housed the kitchen, along the covered walkway to the back porch and from there into the dining room. Our Negroes had been gone for over a year, and we did everything for ourselves. We never went into the fields, however, and they were weed-grown and brown.

Boots made a kind of thunder on the walkway, and on the porch above me. Then I heard men talking in the dining room, not respectfully as the regulars talked, but harsh and demanding, at least until after they'd finished eating what was to have been my supper and Mother's. After that they sounded kind of sly and wheedling, although I couldn't make out what they were saying. Every now and then one of them would laugh at something another had said.

I heard the sound of a scuffle, then the crash the table

made in falling. After that I heard the heavy thump of a body, and a loud, steady cursing. I made out words I'd heard before but wouldn't dare lay my own tongue to.

Then my mother screamed.

I was almighty scared. I'd have given anything to have just lain there shivering and waiting until they went away. But I found myself crawling out from under the porch.

I'd heard Mother scream when someone was hurt. I'd heard her shriek with joy when good news came about the war. But I'd never heard her scream just this way before. There was terror, and disgust, and hate all mixed up in it until it made goose pimples stand out on my arms and made my stomach turn into a cold knot inside me.

I forgot about her telling me to stay put no matter what happened. I crawled out from under the porch and ran into the dining room.

There were three men. You got used to seeing dirty men, tired men, ragged and unshaven men. These were worse than most. I could smell them the minute I stepped into the room.

They all had beards that were ragged from being trimmed with a knife. They wore parts of Northern uniforms, but they weren't regulars any more, you could tell that. Deserters, maybe, who now made a business out of looting.

One of them was flat on his back on the floor, his mouth hanging open and his yellowed, worn-out stubs of teeth showing. Near his head lay the iron cooking pot my mother had hit him with.

One of the others was struggling with her, and the third was sitting in a chair, picking his teeth with a sharpened match and grinning in a way that made me turn cold.

I don't know what I thought I could do. I just lost my head. I remember running at the man who was struggling with Mother, and kicking and biting and scratching him, trying to make him let her go. The man in the chair got up and grabbed me, and I fought him too until he got mad and whacked me on the side of the head with his hand.

I skidded across the floor until my head hit the oak baseboard. After that I don't remember anything. . . .

Coming to was a slow, gradual thing, during which I seemed to recall the sounds of hammer and saw, and afterwards a long silence. When full consciousness returned, I realized that I was upstairs on the bed. The house was quiet and dark.

All that had happened came back to me like a bad dream, and I got up and wandered downstairs to look for Mother. I was scared and shaking because the three men might still be around. My head was splitting, but I knew I had to find her and see if she was all right. A lamp was burning in the room at the foot of the stairs.

When I got to the bottom, I stopped.

There was a man in the room, dressed in the ragged gray of the Confederacy. His uniform was dirty and he needed a shave. His eyes were red, as though he hadn't slept for a long time. A great, tawny mustache swept down and out from his mouth. His nose was a hawk's nose and his face reminded me of the sharp blade of an ax.

There was something vaguely familiar about him. He

said, "Jeff, you all right?"

Anger was in his eyes, smoldering and terrible. It was more than anger. It was wrath, such as God might display as his lightning bolt destroyed the world for its sins.

I stood as still as I could, knowing him all of a sudden from the picture that hung over our mantel. He wasn't much like the picture, or I'd have recognized him sooner; he was thinner, and more tired looking. But he was my father all right—my father, Rob King, captain in the army of the CSA, come home at last.

He seemed to be in kind of a daze. He had a Bible in one hand, and a shovel in the other, and there was fresh, damp dirt sticking to the shovel.

I started to shake violently, and remember being ashamed because I did. I knew I was going to blubber in a minute. I said, "I'm all right, I guess."

Then all of a sudden, I was running toward him. Bible and shovel clattered to the floor as he opened his arms. They folded around me so tight I had to gasp for breath. My tears let go.

Pa's voice was as tight as the twang of a fiddlestring. "You done your best, didn't you, boy?" and I knew he was the one who had found me, out cold there on the dining-room floor.

Pa was talking, as much to himself as to me. "The war's over. Lee has surrendered at Appomattox Courthouse. Four years. Four damn long years, an' we lost." He put me down and went over to stare into the darkness outside the window. "There's nothin' left. Nothin'." He turned and looked around the room, blackened by a fire that had almost taken the whole house a year before. His face twisted. "I ain't stayin' here. I can't now."

I stopped crying, maybe because his agony was so much greater than mine. But every once in a while I'd choke, and the sound would come out like a sob. Except for that the room was still as a grave. After a long time, Pa said, "You an' me are goin' on a trip."

I didn't want to leave, but I didn't dare argue. He said, "This is finished anyway. The land is mortgaged beyond a man's ability to pay back without the men to work it. The house is looted and wrecked until it's only a shell. Out west, we can start new and clean. But I'll tell you somethin', boy. From now on, I'll look after my own. Nobody's ever goin' to take anything from me again. Nobody!"

He sat down in a chair and put his head down into his hands. I thought he was crying, but he wasn't. He was just shaking. He kept saying over and over, "Four years. Four years and nobody to help her. I didn't know it was like this. I just didn't know. Damn! Damn it to hell! An hour sooner. God, if I'd just got here an hour sooner!"

He straightened up and looked at me. He said, "You go on out an' hold my horse. I'll be out in a minute."

Maybe he forgot for a minute what was in the dining room. I heard his voice behind me as I ran out, the curt, commanding voice I recalled vaguely from the days when he was drilling volunteers on our front lawn before they all went away to fight, "Jeff! Don't go out that way!"

But I was already in the dining room.

There is something about dead men that tell you right off they're dead. The three lay there on the floor, all limp and sprawled out. I noticed, in the quick glance I got, that one of them had a round, bluish hole right between his eyes.

Then Pa grabbed me up and carried me out the back door. He set me down, pointed at his big sorrel horse and said, "Hold him until I come out."

I stroked the big horse's neck. I noticed that his hip bones stuck out and even in what light there was from the lamp in the dining room, I could count his ribs.

Pa wasn't gone long. He came out and tossed me up to the saddle. He mounted behind me and we rode away. After a while a red glow touched the horse's head before me, and looking back, I saw what caused it. Our house was a mass of flames.

I couldn't understand, that night, why he'd burned our house, or why we had to run in the night like criminals. I know now that killing a Union soldier, even a deserter, was an offense a man was likely to get hanged for, no matter what the provocation. And Pa had killed three.

We traveled all night, and slept the next day in some brush near a small stream. It was April and the nights were warm, so maybe my shivering was from something besides cold.

Again we traveled all night. I missed Mother and I'd cry for her sometimes when I knew Pa was sleeping. I wanted to go back, but I was afraid to leave Pa. I guess I knew she was dead, but I didn't seem able to comprehend it. I thought if I could just get back there everything would be the same as before. I'd remember our house burning, and the Bible, and the fresh dirt on the shovel Pa'd had when I first saw him, but those things weren't real. My memories of the house, and of Mother, were.

We kept going, day after day, week after week. After we crossed the Mississippi we stopped traveling by night. Pa got rid of his uniform and got some other clothes, linsey-woolsey pants and a blue shirt and a high-crowned hat with a narrow brim that looked strange on him after the flop-brimmed cavalry hat he'd worn before.

He pushed himself and he pushed his horse almost beyond endurance. I don't remember ever being as tired as I was on that trip. Days, I'd drowse behind him in the saddle, and nights I'd sleep like a log.

The plain stretched before us, rolling and green from spring rains. I had never seen so much country in one place before. It seemed as though you could see for a thousand miles.

Sometimes the plain was dotted with the chocolate-colored forms of buffalo, sometimes with the white canvas tops of a wagon train, winding like a serpent across its undulating vastness. Sometimes we'd see a band of Indians galloping along in the distance, and at these times Pa would hunt cover in some brushy ravine or dry wash.

The yucca blossomed, sending up its spires of pale yellow blooms. Wild flowers splashed the plain with brightness, rivaling the blue of the sky, the red of each day's setting sun.

We lived on wild meat, and sometimes Pa would leave

me at night and go on a foraging expedition. Those times he usually came back with chicken, or ham, or potatoes. Lee's surrender at Appomattox Courthouse hadn't changed the world for Pa. He was still at war, only now he was at war with the whole world.

Fortunately, he never got caught—fortunately for those he foraged from, for he still carried his old Dance Brothers and Park percussion revolver and he could draw and shoot it with a speed that never ceased to amaze me. Nights, he'd melt lead over the coals of the campfire and mold his own .44 caliber bullets. He always kept his pouch full and he always had plenty of caps and powder.

Worst of it all for me was the loneliness. Pa was strange and withdrawn, never talking to me at all. He'd only tell me what to do and what not to do.

I grew like a weed that summer. Maybe it was the change from the fever-ridden, swampy country around home. Maybe it was the high, dry air of the plains. Or maybe it was just eating. Pa was a good forager and we never missed a meal nor got up from one hungry.

He avoided people, and when a chance meeting came about unexpectedly, Pa was curt and unfriendly.

I don't know what my father was looking for that summer, or what he expected to find. A boy soon forgets the pain of loss and finds it hard to understand how enduring that pain can be to a man. A father can replace a mother in a boy's heart, but a boy can scarcely replace a wife. Pa was bitter, and time didn't change that.

He seemed to grow in stature as I grew, but I know he only filled out. Food in the Confederate Army had been scarce, and now, eating regularly and fully, he became broader and stronger, but he did not stop brooding and the pain never left his ice-blue eyes. Sometimes I'd catch him looking at me in the strangest way, almost as though he hated me. Usually when I did catch him, he'd look ashamed, and afterward would be unusually kind to me for several days. I know now that he did hate me sometimes, not because of anything I had done, but because I looked like Mother and kept reminding him of her. He wanted so desperately to rid himself of that torturing memory, particularly the memory of the way he'd found her.

Midsummer came, and sometimes it seemed that we were in a kind of hell. The sky turned a brassy color, and the sun beat down pitilessly with never a cloud to shield it until I thought the whole world was afire, and that we'd dry up like the water dogs I'd sometimes caught back home and carelessly left in a box without water.

We were in a strange land, a desert of vast distances, of rising escarpments on the horizon, of mirage, of scrub brush and cactus. We grew used to the buzz of the rattler, to the sight of tiny, incredibly fast lizards. We became accustomed to flash floods roaring down the coulees when there wasn't a cloud in sight and hadn't been for days, except over the blue mountains on the horizon.

Yet for all its discomforts, it was that summer the land took a hold on me, a hold it still has and which will never be broken. I grew to love its blue coolness in early morning before the glittering sun poked its rim above the eastern horizon. I grew to love it in early dusk, when orange and purple and every other shade imaginable splashed the landscape like a careless artist's brush. I grew to love even its dry heat, its wildlife, its tangy, wild smell.

The war years had bred in Pa a wariness that seemed to sharpen here. He avoided parties of raiding Indians with uncanny skill. I can recall many times hiding in some brush or a deep, dry wash, and watching them ride past, so close you could smell their wild and rancid odor, so close you could see the oily shine of sweat on their swarthy painted faces. I grew to know their accouterments, and I could tell an Apache from a Comanche, and Arapahoe from a Cheyenne, a Sioux from a Kiowa.

What with the constant traveling all summer, I'd grown muscular and tough as whang leather. But there came a time when the traveling tired and discouraged me, and I longed to stop and stay somewhere.

We had camped for the night on the bank of one of the dry rivers so common in the Southwest. At its edge were two scrubby cottonwoods, and it was beside one of these that Pa reined in and dismounted. The river consisted of a foot-wide trickle in the middle of a half-mile-wide river bed of dry sand. He said, "This'll do for tonight, Jeff."

Jeff is short for Jefferson—Jefferson Davis King. I believe I was one of the first Southern children to be named after the distinguished president of the CSA, for I was born at a time when he was Secretary of War in the Cabinet of President Franklin Pierce.

I got down and started to unsaddle. I had a horse of my

own by this time and we had a pack mare too. Maybe the weariness of constant traveling showed in me, although I always tried to conceal it. Pa looked at me and appeared really to notice me for the first time since we'd left home.

I'd never seen his face so soft before and I never did again. Probably that's the reason it sticks in my memory. He said, "I can't outrun it, can I, Jeff?"

Of course I didn't know what he was talking about.

He said, "All right. We're through running, and this is as good a place as any to stop. You don't need Negroes to run cattle. You need yourself to begin with and later you need a few riders. This is free land, Jeff. It belongs to the man who takes it, to the man who can hold it against the Indians and anyone else who comes along. You reckon you and me can hold it?"

I said, "I reckon we can."

"How much you figure we ought to take for a start?"

"Enough for a house?"

He laughed. He threw back his great head and roared. And suddenly I found myself remembering the way he'd used to laugh before the war. I had a vague memory of our house filled to overflowing with guests in fancy silk dresses and broadcloth suits, and Negroes moving about with food and drink, white-coated, smiling. I could remember my father's great roaring laugh, echoing through the house so that I could hear it even upstairs in bed.

He clapped me on the back. "More than that, Jeff. We'll go back to the water hole where we nooned today. That's where the house will stand. And we'll take every damned bit of land we can see in all directions. Later, maybe we'll take more." His face sobered and the look in his eyes was suddenly frightening. "But by God nobody's ever going to take any of it away from me."

His eyes in that instant were like hot blue flames. I guess I was puzzled at the time, but I understand him better now. He'd gone away to war to fight for something he'd believed in. Returning, with the war lost and his cause with it, he'd found my mother dead because he had not been with her. He'd made himself a criminal avenging her, and had thereby lost our home. No wonder looking out for his own had become an obsession.

And yet this philosophy did not extend to his fellow-men, because he took from whomever he pleased. I'll give him credit, though. He never ran from any man, or from any thing, as long as he lived.

Chapter Two

I MUST HAVE MATURED very fast during our summer of traveling, because today I remember clearly everything of consequence that happened after we sank our tenuous roots beside that water hole.

For a while we slept on the ground, the way we were accustomed to doing, while Pa and I made adobe bricks from mud and water and dry grass. When he judged we had enough, we began to lay them up, using adobe mud as mortar. A door in one side, a tiny window in the other. Two long slits in the bare walls to be used as rifle ports. We laid up the four walls, and when they were finished we rode to the distant mountains for poles.

Time wasn't important. But long before the days grew cool we had skidded enough poles from the mountain slopes to roof our house. The door and window frames were made from oak timbers salvaged from a broken, abandoned wagon we found graying in the sun. Hinges were leather, and hardware was laboriously shaped over the coals of a campfire and beaten into shape against a rock.

Only when the house was finished did Pa begin to think of cattle. We started south, but this time he did not take me with him. He left me with a Mexican family along his route.

He was gone a month, during which time I learned to speak Spanish. When he returned, he had a raw-looking, half-healed bullet scar in the strong muscles of his shoulder and a herd of eighty cows and three bulls, besides the calves that were running with the cows.

I never asked how he got the cattle. I suppose I knew. They bore a brand which I have since forgotten, but that never seemed to bother him. We drove them home, put our own K Diamond brand on them and turned them loose.

That first year was a year of building. The winter was mild. We made a trip to a settlement called Arriola fifty miles away, and Pa spent the last of his money for tools and wagon and harness for the horses. When we got back, we built a horse corral out of adobe bricks, an enormous thing that enclosed part of the water hole, and building it, I know he was thinking of Indian attacks, for we could have forted up in the corral as easily as we could in the house.

Fortunately the Indians let us alone that first year. And when they did begin to bother us, we were more than ready for them.

Pa made another trip south in the spring, and when he returned the second time he had over three hundred cattle and a Mexican vaquero named Manuel Garcia y Ferrera. He was a thin, slight man almost a head shorter than my father. He wore an enormous black sombrero, tall-crowned, floppy-brimmed, with a snakeskin for a band around its crown. He wore tight leather pants and high-heeled boots and spurs that had rowels like great silver cartwheels. He had a black vest trimmed with silver con-chas.

His black eyes were never serious. They sparkled with a devil of mocking merriment, as though he found the world too ridiculous to take seriously.

Manuel was the first man I had seen who wore a gun the way he did. It sagged low at his side, as though the belt which supported it were too loose, and a leather thong through a ring in the bottom of the holster went around his leg and tied there.

Manuel was company for me. He was not remote, as Pa was, but had a carefree nature that made me like him immediately. He was always humming or singing some snatch of song, and his voice was pleasant if somewhat high-pitched and reedy. When he'd smile his white teeth flashed against his swarthy skin like the snow on the dis-tant brown slopes of the mountains, and the skin around his eyes would wrinkle up into a thousand fascinating lines.

When Pa was gone, we'd often sit in the sun before the house and Manuel would show me how to braid a strong, soft lariat from strips of hide. Or we'd walk on the prairie, and he'd teach me the tracks of the different animals.

Pa hadn't been home from bringing the cattle and Manuel more than a month or so when one day we saw the dust of approaching riders to the south.

At once the interest of both Pa and Manuel centered on the riders, and Pa seemed concerned over the presence of one of our cows at the water hole.

The riders came closer. There were three of them, and they were dressed much as Manuel was. I judged they were Mexicans too.

Pa said shortly, "Jeff, go into the house and shut the door."

It was the tone he used when he'd brook no argument. I looked at his face, which was as bleak as winter wind. I wanted to stay outside, for visitors were almost unheard of, but I took that one look at his stony face and went into the house.

Pa must have weighed over two hundred pounds that spring. He was tall and solid, every ounce of him muscle and bone. His face had darkened under the desert sun until it was almost as dark as oiled latigo leather. He still wore his great, tawny mustache cavalry style, sweeping down and away from his hawklike nose and curling up slightly at the ends. Today he had a golden stubble of whiskers on his face.

He inspired tremendous awe in me as he stood there, eyes as blue as the cloudless sky, but hard as gun steel for all of that.

Manuel lounged beside him, a carefree smile on his lips that didn't fool anybody, least of all me. I couldn't see the tenseness that was in him, but I could feel it.

For some reason I began to sweat as I watched through the crack in the partly open door, yet even while I was sweating, I felt cold. I knew trouble was coming, and I was as scared as I'd been that night I hid under the porch and heard my mother scream.

The three riders came into the yard. They didn't look at Pa or Manuel. Instead they rode over to the cow at the water hole. I could hear their murmuring voices, but couldn't tell what they said.

After what seemed an eternity they turned and rode over to face Pa and Manuel. One of them, the old one, flashed a smile at Pa, a smile that was like Manuel's in that it didn't fool anyone. Like a sheathed knife, its sharpness was hidden, but you knew the sharpness was there anyway. The old one said, "*Buenas dias, señores.* You have branded one of our cows by mistake."

Pa's voice was harsh. "You misread the brand, seems like." The Mexican's courtesy didn't fool him any more than it did me. Pa knew what they had come for and it wasn't to stand in the sun pleasantly passing the time of day. They were only trying to throw him off guard for a few moments.

I didn't think what I was doing. Crossing the room and taking down my father's old Maynard carbine was almost automatic. The gun was a breech-loading single-shot and it was always loaded. I went to the door and poked the muzzle out.

The Mexican dropped his courtesy like a cloak. His eyes turned hard and he stopped smiling. He spat the words, "Thieves! We trailed over two hundred head. We have seen more than twenty bearing our brand and your brand too."

Pa didn't give an inch. "Mister, you're a damn liar!"

I was getting a little sick at my stomach because I knew what was going to happen. All five of them out in the yard were as tense as a rattlesnake just before he strikes. I knew Pa was in the wrong but I knew where I had to stand anyway. If I didn't they'd kill him or they'd take him away and put him in prison. Either way I'd be left alone. So I pulled the gun up to my shoulder and took a bead on the chest of the old one. I steadied the heavy gunbarrel on the jamb of the door.

I didn't say a word. I just knew that when that Mexican grabbed for his gun, he was going to get a bullet in his chest.

Maybe I made some small sound, or maybe some sixth sense made the Mexican's eyes dart to me, swiftly as the small orange and black tongue of a snake.

He grabbed for his gun, but I guess not knowing in his own mind whether he was going to shoot me or Pa slowed him down. I tried to tighten my finger on the trigger, but it was as if I was paralyzed. I couldn't do it.

Pa and Manuel appeared to crouch the way a cougar does before he springs. Their guns appeared in their hands with instant swiftness and shots crackled like a string of Chinese firecrackers.

Manuel held his gun in his right hand and with the left kept fanning the hammer. Each time he did the gun puffed bluish powdersmoke and bucked a little in his hand. Pa used his gun differently, thumbing back the hammer for each shot. But there wasn't much difference in speed between the two.

The old one fell first, his own gun hardly out of the holster. One of the others got off a single shot that kicked up dust five or six feet behind Pa. Then he fell as his horse whirled away from the roaring guns and blinding smoke. The third started to gallop away, but Manuel shot him in the back and he fell too. His horse galloped for a hundred yards and then stopped.

I was too dazed to move for a long time. It couldn't have been as long as it seemed, because Manuel and Pa still had their guns in their hands when I opened the door and went out. I still carried the carbine.

There was a thin cloud of powdersmoke in the yard. The breeze drifted it over me and filled my nostrils until I wanted to cough. I noticed the old one, lying face up on the ground, and I noticed the round, blue hole between his eyes.

Memory came back with a rush. I was back in the house at home, and I was hearing my mother scream, seeing the dead face of that Yankee deserter at the same time. I was smelling the cloud of powdersmoke that drifted down the wind from the woods near our house and hearing the musket fire and the distant boom of a cannon.

I started toward Pa, wanting him to hold his arms out to me as he'd done on that day so long ago.

Perhaps something about this stirred his own memory, for his face twisted with pure anguish and a great, long shudder went through his body. He looked at me, his eyes cold and filled with pain.

I think I knew in that instant how much of my mother was in my appearance, because he looked away from me quickly as though he had been looking into the accusing eyes of mother. There was never any real closeness between us afterward.

I know he felt guilty that day. During the war he had killed because it was his duty and because he was fighting for something he had believed in. At our house that night he had killed for vengeance, in the crazy fury of grief and outrage. This time was different, and both he and I knew it. He had killed today because he had been a thief. He had killed three men whose only crime was to run down the man who had stolen their cattle.

Manuel was watching me, and for once the merriment was gone from his eyes. He said, "Rob, you better talk to heem."

Pa started to say something to me. Then he looked helplessly at Manuel. "There's nothin' to say. He understands what happened." He looked at me and tried again, and again gave up. At last he said, not looking at me, "He's old enough to make his own judgments. Let him alone."

That was all that was ever said about it, then or later. But Pa made no more trips south. . . .

The days slipped past, but there was something changed in our relationship. I had wondered if he hated me before, but now I knew he did. He drove me mercilessly and he drove himself and Manuel even harder. We rode from dawn to dark each day, even during the howling storms that came down out of the vague distances to the north.

We checked the cattle's drift, although my father apparently intended to claim everything north of that dry, wide river and as far as the escarpment they called El Espalto de Cerdo. We kept them fairly close to home, where we could keep track of them.

When spring came we branded. I was twelve that year, and growing tall and stringy. But for all my stringiness, I was strong and could ride as good as either Manuel or Pa.

Manuel had taught me to use a lariat so well that I seldom missed a throw. Manuel would hold the cattle bunched, and I'd ride into them and rope a calf. I'd drag him out past the fire, where Pa would throw him. Pa would throw off my loop and I'd ride out and take Manuel's place while Manuel rode in and branded. We could have used another man, which would have saved us time, but Pa didn't figure we were ready for one and he wouldn't hire one until we were.

Pa had mapped out the building of our ranch in his mind as carefully as a cavalry commander maps his campaign strategy. He'd needed land and he'd taken it. He needed cattle, and he'd taken them. But heaven help whoever tried to take something from Pa.

Now, Pa needed time for the cattle to multiply. But he had to fight for every year of it.

Chapter Three

NOT ALL MY MEMORIES deal with the violence of those first few years, nor of the drudgery and hard work that accompanied it.

I recall lying on my back and staring at the clouds marching across the sky—the miracle of spring; new-born calves spooking away from me as I rode along, their ridiculous tails straight up in the air like tiny banners; the wobble-legged colts; a fawn lying beside a clump of brush, still as death and thinking he was unseen.

I've heard that a fawn has no smell, and so can go undetected by wolves and coyotes unless they step right over him. It seems unlikely, but what else can explain their remarkable ability to remain uncaught?

When I was fifteen, Pa and Manuel took off for Arriola with a small herd of cattle. It was midsummer. They said they were going for supplies, but something about their manner made me suspect otherwise. On trips for supplies I always went along, yet this time I was definitely told I couldn't go.

I watched them ride out, resentful and restless. I'd watched the tension build in Pa the last few years. Being young, I didn't understand what it was. I do now. He was a strong and virile man. He'd steeped himself in work to forget the cravings natural in a man, but he'd reached a point where work no longer stilled them.

I sulked around the house for a while. Then I went out and wandered around the yard. Pa had corraled the horses for safekeeping, since he'd promised to be back before morning. I climbed up on the adobe corral wall and sat there staring at them.

Dust in the distance caught my attention. Pretty soon it wasn't just dust any more, but a small party of Indians.

I scooted for the house and barred the door. I took down the old Maynard carbine.

I watched from the window. I couldn't keep my knees from knocking together, and my hands were clammy.

It was a small party of Apaches. One of them had a rifle, the others bows. They were all young men, the youngest being scarcely older than myself. Their hair was shoulder-length, bound around their heads with red bands of cloth. They were naked to the waist, and wore filthy breechclouts. Their legs were encased to the knees with the blunt-nosed moccasins peculiar to the Apache. Their faces and chests were daubed with red paint that sweat had smeared until it ran raggedly across their dusty bodies.

They guided their ponies with their knees, although the horses wore simple, rawhide bridles.

They paid no more attention to the house than they did to any other part of the landscape, and from this I guessed they had been waiting, and had seen father and Manuel ride out. They thought the house was deserted.

The horses in the corral were what they were interested in. They reined in leisurely beside the corral wall and I could hear them talking among themselves in Indian, now pointing at one or another of our horses approvingly.

I knew they intended to take the horses, and I knew, too, that they wouldn't leave without going through the house. There was one gun among them. They wouldn't pass up a chance to add another to it.

Scared or not, I had to make some kind of show. I leaned the carbine against the wall and ran and got cartridges and primers. I put them together on the table, where they'd be handy for reloading.

I went back to the window and poked the carbine out. They had the horses out of the corral now, and were milling around in the yard, trying to get the horses headed right.

I took a bead on the Indian with the rifle, probably the head man—and for the second time in my life I failed my father and failed myself. I couldn't hold the gun on him and squeeze off the trigger at the same time. If the sights were on, my finger wouldn't pull.

Shaking with frustration, I let the muzzle waver off and pulled the trigger.

I didn't wait to see what happened. I ran as fast as I could to the table and reloaded. Then I rushed over to one of the rifle ports and without even bothering to aim, fired again.

I heard their high yells of surprise. They'd been so sure the house was deserted. Now they didn't know whether they were up against one man or half a dozen.

I got off four shots, the last at their retreating backs more than a quarter of a mile away.

Our horses were gone, and I hadn't drawn blood from the thieves. I sat down in the middle of the floor and bawled like a baby. I thought of the anger Pa would show me for being so soft. I made up my mind I wouldn't tell him.

Let him think it was fear and nervousness that made me miss. Let him think anything. Actually, I suppose missing saved my life. The Apaches were glad to get off with the horses and whole skins. But if I'd killed or wounded one of them they'd probably have made a fight of it.

I think that night was the longest of my whole life. I didn't sleep until gray began to outline the eastern horizon. All night long I lay and called myself a coward, and sweated, and chilled, and dreaded my father's return even while I longed for it so that I could get this torment off my mind.

I envied my father, and I hated him. He was a man, one who could do what was needed. He'd have killed three or four of those Apaches, and he'd have saved the horses.

He came riding in at sunup with Manuel trailing him. Both of them were red-eyed, but Pa was grinning as if he were darned pleased with himself—until he saw the empty corral.

He let out a shout. Manuel came up to him and Pa pointed at the empty corral. Manuel began questing around the yard like a hound looking for a trail.

I was shaking worse than I'd shook while the Apaches were in the yard. Manuel said, "Seven, Señor Rob. 'Paches. They go south."

Pa turned and stared at the house. I saw a look of stark

fear on his face, the like of which I'd never seen before. Pale and sweating, he came bursting in the door.

When he saw me there facing him from the window, he stopped cold. "Jeff! Holy God, boy, why didn't you sing out? I thought—"

I could feel my lower lip trembling. I blurted, "I never hit a one of them. I couldn't—" I'd intended to let him have it straight, but he cut me off.

"Hell no, you couldn't. Seven of 'em! God, I'd a been scared too."

Manuel muttered, "Good thing Jeff no hit heem." He made a gesture across his throat with his index finger.

Pa stood there for a minute. Then he said, "Come on, Jeff. We're going after them." He had that hard, cold look to his face and his eyes were afire with fury.

I pulled on my boots and followed him out the door. Manuel went down to the water hole and laid flat on his belly while he drank. His face was pale when he got up. He looked apologetically at Pa, then bent doubled and vomited on the ground.

He mounted. I climbed on Pa's horse, and Pa swung up behind me. Riding out, Pa said to Manuel, "Let 'em have those horses and they'll be back every six months for more. But stop 'em this time and they'll give us a wide berth."

Manuel shrugged expressively. "Perhaps." He never argued with Pa.

I'd been pretty quiet up to now. I'd felt bad because I hadn't acquitted myself better while the Indians were taking the horses. But now, suddenly, I knew what Pa was going to do. He was going to hunt those Indians until he'd killed every one of them. He'd pick them off one by one until the odds were reduced to a point where he could get them all, and take the horses back.

I said, "Pa, you ain't goin' to do no more killin'."

I could feel him stiffen. For a moment we rode in silence while I had a chance to consider the enormity of what I'd done. Then he reined the horse to a halt. He swung off and stood on the ground looking up at me.

He was flabbergasted. He didn't know what to say. I didn't either. I could feel the blood draining from my face. But I stared him straight in the eye. He growled, "You goddamn little rooster, mind your tongue with me."

I said, "Don't cuss at me. All you know is killin'. I guess maybe I stand up to you and you want to kill me too, huh?"

His face got a brick-red color and then it turned gray. He looked like he had that time standing before the house waiting for the three Mexicans to draw, tense as a coiled rattler. His eyes had their flaming look and seemed to burn a hole through me, the way a branding iron burns a hole in a dry hide.

All of a sudden his whole body went limp. He said, "Get down, Jeff. It's time we talked."

I don't know what had got into me. I said, "Sure, talk until I come around to your way of thinkin'. But I ain't never goin' to come around. It ain't been so long that I've forgot Ma. She wouldn't hold with all this killin'."

I'd slid down off the horse while I was talking. Now, suddenly, Pa's hand swung and slapped the side of my face. There was so much force in the blow it knocked me off my feet. It sounded like a pistol shot, and the whole side of my face turned numb.

I got up and stood looking at him. I didn't say anything, but I've a notion all the things I was feeling were right there in my eyes.

I saw many things in my father's face in those few seconds. Shame, because he had slapped me, and because in his heart he felt I was right. Anger to be balked and defied. Pain, because the impression was there in him that he was not facing me, but Mother.

Manuel's voice intruded, "Señor Rob, maybe we can get the horses away without killing."

"No!"

I knew I was crowding my luck, staring at him so defiantly. I looked away. Pa said, "We're like an old cow that's ringed by wolves. We've got land that we hold only because we're willing to fight for it. We've got cattle scattered from one end of it to the other, and by God we can't guard every cow. But we can put another kind of guard around everything that the damned wolves will respect. We can show 'em that whoever steals from K Diamond dies. Show 'em one bit of weakness and they'll pull us down."

Manuel said softly, "*Es verdad,* Señor Jeff."

Pa said, "There ain't a cowman in the country that didn't make his start usin' a long rope." He knew I was thinking of the three Mexicans he and Manuel had killed and who were buried in unmarked graves a quarter of a mile behind our house.

It was all the explaining Pa ever did. He looked at me for a minute more. Then he said, "I'd give you your choice about going along, but with one band of Apaches this far north, I figure there might be others. I ain't going to leave you at the house alone." He nodded his head toward his horse. "Get up."

I knew when I was beat, and I was beat now. I got up on Pa's horse and he swung up behind.

We rode hard all that day, with Manuel a little ahead, tracking. Most times, the trail of the stolen horses and the Apaches was easy to follow, so we made good time. We didn't stop until full dark.

There wasn't much talk, except for Manuel's. He made an almost desperate effort to get things back to normal, but neither Pa nor I responded.

Our first camp was a dry one, with nothing to eat. I remembered that Pa and Manuel had gone to town yesterday, for supplies, as they put it. They didn't even have a can of beans behind their saddles.

I was so tired that I went to sleep instantly. It seemed only a minute before Manuel was shaking me.

I rolled out and we saddled up and rode again, picking up the trail by the first faint light of dawn.

At sunup, Manuel came back from scouting ahead. "We have got to eat, Señor Rob," he said. "I think a shot will be safe."

Pa nodded, and we split up, leaving the trail but paralleling it. After a while we heard a shot, and riding that way, found that Manuel had killed an antelope.

He had it gutted by the time we reached him and was

wiping his knife blade on his leather pants. I was hungry enough to chance eating the meat with the animal heat still in it, but I didn't say anything. Manuel slung the carcass on behind his saddle and we rode on.

At noon we halted beside a small stream and broiled some of the antelope over a small fire. Afterward we went on.

Again we rode all day, but at evening the tracks of the Apaches were much fresher and we knew we were gaining. We had to reach those Apaches before they joined the main band.

In spite of myself I was being caught up with the excitement of the chase. Except for Pa's avowed intention to kill the Indians, I might have enjoyed it.

About midmorning the next day we came to the top of a low escarpment and could look ahead for twenty miles. A dust cloud raised out there, and Manuel uttered a grunt of satisfaction. "There they are, Señor Rob."

I looked at my father. What I'd expected to see, I don't quite know. Probably I looked to see lust for the kill, or enjoyment, or anticipation of some sort. I saw none of those things, and the fact that I didn't was something of a disappointment.

And I realized something quite suddenly. This was a job to him and nothing else. My father was one of those people whom ambition drives incessantly. He had a dream of something so big that no one could ever take it from him. This was simply one of the things he knew he had to do to build it, and keep it.

Had it not been for the war, and my mother's death, he

might have remained back home, a gentleman planter content with what he had and making no particular effort to enlarge upon it. But that had been changed the night of my mothers' death, the night he killed the three Union deserters.

Even now, I doubted if he wanted what he was building here for itself alone. Loss had simply wrought a curious kind of need within him to compensate for what he had lost. Everything had been taken from him in a single night through no fault of his own. Perhaps subconsciously he felt that he could never again know contentment until he had replaced it.

In the saddle behind me he said, "Jeff?" and I knew he'd put me down here to wait until it was over if I asked him to. I said, "I'll go along."

He touched heels to his horse's sides and we rode out briskly, circling to cut in ahead of the leisurely traveling band of Apaches.

Chapter Four

ALL THAT DAY WE RODE. At nightfall we halted, and Manuel went out on a scout.

We waited for two hours, while the tension of waiting mounted in both of us. At last Manuel returned with the unconsciously low-voiced comment. "They're camped two miles west of here. I figure they'll move into that broken country ahead of us tomorrow. I scouted it and there's only one decent way through it. They don't know we're tailing them, so we maybe can lay an *emboscada*."

Nobody had bothered to ask me about the Indians, so they didn't know the Apaches had only one rifle amongst them. I thought of it now, and wondered whether I should say anything.

I couldn't see how it could matter what I did. If Pa had his way, the Apaches were going to die anyway. I said, "There's only one rifle in that bunch of Apaches. The rest of them have got bows and arrows."

There was a kind of fatalism in me now, as though nothing I said or did could change the course of destiny. My father's iron will and the blue flame in his eyes were a destiny in themselves. He had the strength and the implacable determination to build what he had set out to build, and build it he would. He squatted there beside our tiny fire and the orange flickering light of the flames cast shadows on his face that made it look like the sharp blade of an axe.

I had a thought which seemed sacrilegious at the time. It was that God must look a great deal like my father looked that night. I wondered what would happen if Father ever came to grips with God.

My telling them about the single gun the Apaches had seemed to make a difference. Pa said, "Then we won't wait to ambush them. We'll hit them tonight."

He scattered the embers of the fire with his boot and stamped them out. He said, "Mount up, Jeff," and I did. He swung up behind me and we started out.

When we were within half a mile of the Indian camp, Manuel halted. He said softly, "Just ahead is a low ridge, Señor Rob. We can leave Jeff there and he can watch in safety."

I opened my mouth to protest, but closed it knowing it was neither sensible nor practical to attack an Indian camp riding double.

I slid off at the top of the ridge and they went on without me. Below me, a quarter of a mile away, I could see the winking fire of the Indians. The Apaches were sure of themselves or they'd have had no fire. They figured it was known they were seven strong, and they didn't expect two white men to have the temerity to attack them.

Straining my eyes, I counted four sleeping forms within the circle of light from the fire. I made out a fifth, sitting up. I guessed the other two were night-herding the horses.

Nervousness began to build in me as I waited for Father and Manuel to hit the camp. Minutes dragged until each one seemed like an hour.

Suddenly I saw the guard beside the campfire leap to his feet. He whirled and the rifle jumped to his shoulder. But he never got a chance to fire. He doubled as though a fist had slammed into his belly. He was still on his feet when the flat sound of the shot reached me, but he was falling. Now the sleeping forms beside the fire came to life, scrambling to get out of the light. One of them seemed to stumble, and an instant later I heard the sound of another shot.

It was panic down there now, pure panic. A third went down, and a fourth, but this one began to crawl, dragging a useless leg behind him.

I began to feel sick at my stomach. I reminded myself that these same Apaches that Pa and Manuel were killing had doubtless wiped out more than one isolated white family, burning and killing and mutilating with no more mercy than Pa was showing them.

Without thinking, I began to run toward the scene below me. Off from the campfire, probably where the horse herd was being held, I heard several more shots.

I knew how they'd planned it then. Pa had probably hit the Indians at the fire while Manuel hit the night-herders.

Something went past me in the darkness, a stooping, running Apache, and behind him, driving his horse hard, came Pa.

For an instant he was silhouetted against the fire, and I saw that his lariat was out and whirling around his head. The loop went out with a sighing sound, and the horse turned immediately at a sharp angle.

The 'Pache let out a high yell, hit the ground with a thump, and then went dragging past me, jerking and jumping like a rag doll on the end of a string.

Pa dragged him up into the firelight. As if the Indian were a calf, Pa jumped out of the saddle and ran over to him. Pa's boot, swinging savagely, kicked the knife out of the Indian's hand. Then Pa was on him, straddling him, tying his hands and feet with a pigging string.

It sounds, telling it, as if Pa had an easy time. He didn't. All the time he was straddling the Indian, the savage was fighting with a desperate kind of fury. But in the end he lay trussed and helpless, while Pa stood over him, looking down and breathing with a hoarse, rasping sound.

Beyond the circle of firelight, I heard Manuel's curse, surprised and sudden, and after that another shot. Manuel came into the light, limping and cursing. The leg of his leather pants was slashed, and turning red with his blood.

I suppose I was awed into immobility by the suddenness of events and perhaps by the play-like quality of the scene before me. But I just stood there in the darkness, unmoving, and watched. I've wished since that I'd stepped forward to where they could see me, because if I had, Pa probably wouldn't have done it.

He fumbled around on his saddle, took something and threw it into the fire. Then he went over and helped Manuel tie up the gash on his leg.

There had been seven Indians, and all were dead save for the one lying trussed on the ground.

Pa finished with Manuel. He hunted around until he found two sticks and then he fished in the fire with them. I saw what he was fishing for now, for he took it, red-hot, from the fire. It was a circular, copper branding iron. Holding it with two sticks, he went over to the Apache. I began to run toward the fire, so shocked my throat seemed to close. I tried to yell, but the sound came out like a weak bleat.

Pa peeled the Apache's breechclout down. Smoke rose, and I heard the sound of the Indian's sharply indrawn breath. I burst into the circle of firelight just as Pa finished. I was shaking and felt as though I were going to be sick. On the Indian's rump Pa had branded an angry-looking HT.

I couldn't speak. Pa looked at Manuel. "Tell him to go back to his people. Tell him to show them the mark of the thief on his rump. Tell him that all Apaches stealing horses from me will be so marked."

I believe even Manuel was awed by my father in that moment. He spoke some Apache gutturals at the Indian. The Indian looked at father with more flaming hatred than I had ever seen in a man's eyes. But it seemed to me there was another quality in the Indian's glance—awe. Probably no one in the history of the Southwest had ever had the temerity to brand an Apache.

Even Manuel looked scared. He said, "Better to kill him, Señor Rob, than to let him go now."

But Pa shook his head. It was plain even to me that one of two things would happen as a result of turning the branded Apache loose. Either he'd bring the whole tribe down on us, or his story would keep them away forever.

The Apache admired courage above all things, and it was quite possible that they would indeed stay off K Diamond, not out of fear but out of admiration for Pa's almost foolhardy courage.

Pa said, "Manuel, catch Jeff a horse. Then you and he can start the horses home. I'll turn this one loose afoot and come after you."

Manuel rode off into the darkness, and after a long while came back with one of our horses for me. Using one of the Apache bridles, and riding bareback, I mounted, and Manuel and I rode out to bunch the horses and start them home. We left the Indian ponies, since they would have slowed us down, what with biting and kicking and fighting our horses.

Pa joined us after a while, and we kept driving steadily, drowsing sometimes as we rode, until we reached home.

As with all things that happened, there was no rehashing of our brush with the Indians. Pa apparently never questioned the right of what he had done, apparently never even thought of it. But it seemed to me that he was piling up a debt that would some day have to be paid.

Chapter Five

PA AND I WERE the first settlers in that part of the territory, but we weren't the last. Others were settling all around us, not close neighbors, but neighbors all the same. Gradually it had got so they'd come riding in to our place before they settled and ask Pa where his boundaries were. His reputation was spreading.

K Diamond stretched across the rolling grassland from the near-dry river to the escarpment of El Espalto de Cerdo. On the west it was bordered by rough badlands, and on the east by the Arriola river, running in a deep canyon surrounded by low, cedar-covered hills.

Martin Longstreet, a tall, gaunt, ugly-faced man of about sixty, settled beyond the escarpment to the north with his herd of two thousand Texas cattle which he'd brought up from the south. Frank Delaney settled to the south of the river, which was named Sand Creek, with his plump, outspoken wife Bess.

Jim Purser and the three Anson brothers took the badlands, and old Mrs. Peckham, with her wild gunfighter son and hard-riding daughter Rose, took the cedar hills on the far side of the Arriola River.

How they heard of our brush with the Apaches, I don't know. I'm sure Manuel didn't talk, and Pa certainly didn't. Perhaps someone found the bodies of the dead Apaches and drew their conclusions from that.

At any rate, a couple of weeks after we got back we were visited by every one of our neighbors except the Anson brothers.

Frank Delaney came first, riding in at noon and eating dinner with us. Sitting around smoking afterward, he brought up the subject, and for once his round, smiling face was serious. "Hear you had a fuss with Apaches, Rob."

Pa nodded. Delaney studied him a moment, then said, "Hear one of 'em got away, travelin' south afoot."

Again Pa nodded. Delaney muttered, "He's liable to bring the whole kit an' kaboodle of 'em down on us."

Pa said, "I thought of it. There's somethin' your sign readin' didn't tell you. That Apache had an HT branded on his butt."

Delaney lost some color. He looked at Pa and growled, "You're either damned smart or a damned fool. Hell, man, I'm right in their path if they come north. I got my wife with me."

"They won't come." Pa sounded as certain as though he were saying, "Rain tomorrow. The feel of it's in the air."

"But that buck you branded—'Paches won't forget a thing like that."

"They'll laugh him out of the band. And they'll stay away."

Arguing with Pa was like arguing with a stone wall. Delaney kept at it for a little while but in the end he left, shaking his head. Jim Purser and Longstreet came in together, grave and a little scared late that afternoon. They gave Pa something to think about.

Longstreet, his ugly old face sombre with worry, said, "I crossed the sign of a rider yesterday. Unshod pony. Mebbe you kept the band off our necks, but I'll bet you a fat cow you see your branded buck again."

Pa laughed, that great, booming laugh of his. Longstreet looked at him strangely and he and Purser got up and went out to their horses in silence. They had scarcely disappeared from sight when Mrs. Peckham and Rose rode in.

Rose stayed outside and she and I stared at each other warily while Mrs. Peckham talked with Pa in the house.

Rose was a leggy girl of thirteen or fourteen. Her hair was black as India ink and she wore it in two long braids that reached almost to her waist. Despite the way she lived in the open, her skin was white, freckled across her nose. A girl was a strange, foreign creature to me, even a boyishly dressed girl like this one.

I didn't know what to say to her, so I said nothing, but I could feel my face getting red. Finally she said, "Ma says them Injuns will come back an' massacree you."

"Huh!" I snorted. "They'll get the same thing they got before if they try it."

"That's what you think. Ma says they'll likely bring the whole band next time."

"I hope they do. I just hope they do. Then we'll get a

chance to fix 'em good."

The way she looked at me, I think she believed we really could. I felt about seven feet tall. I noticed a difference between Rose and me, even though we were dressed the same. She didn't look hard and stringy the way a boy does, but soft and warm.

I felt my face getting hot again and wished I were somewhere else. Then I heard my father's booming laugh and he and Mrs. Peckham came out into the yard, with Pa still laughing as though the branded Apache were too humiliated a character to be taken seriously.

But Pa didn't laugh three days later when he and I rode down into a little hollow and found three fat steers shot to death and already bloating from the sun.

His eyes flashed fire and his jaw tightened. His mouth became a thin, straight line of fury. We rode back to the house and got Manuel, and until dark trailed the unshod hoofprints that went away from that small hollow.

We weren't more than ten miles from the house when dark caught up with us, so we rode in and Pa said we'd pick up the trail tomorrow.

Next day the trail led us to a mare, heavy with foal, dead of a bullet in the brain. There was a hunk of meat cut out of her hindquarter.

We trailed that Apache until we were ready to drop. All told, he killed five horses and more than fifty cattle. Then, as suddenly as he had appeared, he disappeared.

Pa said he'd worn his vengeance out. Manuel thought otherwise. I was so relieved to stop trailing him that I just didn't care. I should have cared, as it turned out, because that Apache was to blame for my being sent away, and for the woman Pa brought from Arriola to live at K Diamond. . . .

A month later, the 'Pache struck again. And again we trailed him until we were red-eyed with weariness.

Maybe the Indian knew what he was doing to Pa and maybe he didn't. But he was hurting Pa as he'd never been hurt before. The Apache was as elusive as a ghost, striking and running, now disappearing into the vast distances to the south until we thought he'd gone for good, now appearing again. I grew used to the sweet-gagging smell of death, and to the pale fury in my father's face. He was short with me, and more than once I saw rebellion flare in Manuel's dark eyes which had lately forgotten to laugh and which were now only narrow slits peering out of a face caked with dust and grime.

Pa had sworn to himself that no one, ever, would take anything from him again. And here was this Indian, branded with an HT for Horse Thief on his rump, taking every day, and wantonly destroying. It was worse than stealing.

Pa reluctantly gave up the chase in the fall long enough to join Longstreet and Delaney and the others on roundup. But the destruction went on, and Pa began to lose weight and to grow thin and haggard with his hatred. I'm sure that year he'd have given the whole of K Diamond to be able to line his sights on the elusive Apache.

He hired a crew in Arriola and sent Manuel with the crew and the cattle to Abilene, and the Apache hunt went on. Once, in November, we got so close to the Indian that he abandoned his horse. But afoot, he was as destructive and a lot more elusive than he was horseback.

Northers came howling down on us from the escarpment of El Espalto de Cerdo, but we huddled in our ragged sheepskins and rode on. With snow on the ground, the Apache would hole up so he wouldn't make tracks, and we'd be hunting a ghost, riding aimlessly, trying to pick up some trail to follow. With the disappearance of the snow and the mud which followed it, the Apache would strike again.

It was during one of these snowstorms that Pa sent me in to Arriola with the new buckboard for supplies.

It was a cold, bleak day, the wind sighing through the tall, spiny greasewood, rippling the dry brown grass until it looked like water.

A band of antelope stared at me curiously from a knoll as I drove along. Cattle stood with their rumps to the wind, their long, shaggy hair whipping in it. A band of horses galloped· along the skyline, tails up in the air, necks arched.

I was driving along, face burrowed into the upturned collar of my sheepskin. I wasn't thinking about the Indian, but of Arriola, and of the excitement of going there all by myself.

The horses spooked, and I sat up straight, tightening the reins and glancing around for whatever it was that had spooked them.

One of them reared, and snorted, and suddenly here came that Apache, rushing at me from a clump of brush at the roadside where he'd materialized as though out of thin air.

Pa had given me his old Dance Brothers and Park percussion revolver, and I had it under my sheepskin, but I had no time even to think of it, much less get it.

The Apache made a flying leap from the ground, a long knife gleaming dully in his hand. His face was thin and ravaged by privation and cold, but it flamed with a hatred of greater intensity even than my father's.

Only those horses, nervous at the wild Indian smell, saved me. They bolted at almost the instant the Apache left the ground to leap upon me. He lit in the buckboard bed like a cat, his knife slashing at me with wicked virulence. But the bolting horses and the resulting jerk of the buckboard threw him off his feet.

I dropped the reins. I should have been scared, I guess, but I just didn't have the time. I whirled around on the buckboard seat, clawing up the skirt of my sheepskin to get at my gun.

I got it out, but I was in an awkward position now, my legs up over the back of the seat, hanging to the seat with one hand and pulling the revolver with the other. The Indian got up, crouched, and leaped at me.

It was purely automatic on my part, putting my booted feet up to fend him off. The knife slashed at my leg and I felt it sting as it went through my pants, but it didn't more than scratch my ankle.

I gave a frantic pull with the hand that gripped the seat, still clinging to the revolver with the other, and tumbled over the seat into the back of the buckboard.

I bowled the Indian over as I did, and he went down

beneath me. Again I felt that knife rip into the back of my sheepskin coat, its sharp edge burning the flesh of my back.

Pa would never have mixed it up with the Indian at all. He'd have sat there on the seat and shot him dead. But a man only does what he does, and sometimes it's not conscious thinking that controls him at all. I never even got the hammer of the gun back. But I used it as a club, and my second blow made the Indian go limp beneath me.

The buckboard was tearing down the two-track road, lurching from side to side, bounding high into the air whenever the wheels would hit a small wash or clump of brush.

I climbed back into the seat and managed to recover the reins. I hauled the horses in to a panting, trembling halt. Then I turned to look at the Indian.

He wore a filthy, ragged breechclout, knee-length moccasins from which the soles were gone, and a white man's thin cotton shirt, once white but now filthy. His face was like a death's head and his skin was almost blue with cold. His breathing was thin and shallow.

This was the scourge of K Diamond, the man my father would almost have given the ranch to be able to kill. Hell, the poor damned critter wouldn't weigh ninety pounds soaking wet.

Pa would have killed him as he lay there with no more compunction than he'd have felt about killing a diamondback. But I felt an overwhelming pity for the Indian. Probably his tribe had cast him out because of the brand and his failure to avenge it. So he'd come back, bent on a vengeance that would earn back his place in the tribe.

The Indian stirred. I crawled back and wrenched the knife out of his hand and threw it out into the brush. Then I took a length of rope that was lying in the back of the buckboard and trussed him up. He came to as I finished, and lay there staring at me with the unblinking hatred, the ugly virulence of a gila monster.

I sat there hesitating for a minute, wondering whether I should go back home with the Indian, or on into town with him. I knew taking him home would be the same as killing him, for Pa wouldn't hesitate an instant. I knew, too, that if I didn't take him home to Pa there was going to be hell to pay.

The Indian commenced to thrash around, fighting the ropes savagely but futilely. At last he quieted, and sweating, lay still. I got the tarpaulin out of the back, and unfolded it. I threw it over him so he wouldn't chill.

Climbing back into the seat, I took the road to Arriola. I won't say I wasn't scared. Half a dozen times I almost turned and went back, but I didn't.

I suppose all through the past five years there had been a growing resentment in me toward Pa. I won't say it wasn't partly jealousy, because I knew it was. He was such a giant of a man in every way that I knew I'd never be quite able to match up to him. As long as I lived he'd ride better than I, shoot better than I, show more raw, cold courage than I. He was never afraid, never doubtful. I guess he just overwhelmed me.

That, perhaps, was the seed of my rebellion. Hauling

the Apache into Arriola and turning him over to the new sheriff there was its first manifestation. And afterward the breach widened year by year, until that final year when death rode the screaming, ice-laden wind that howled down out of the north, killing everything in its path.

The fact that the Indian died in jail of lung fever as he waited for the military authorities to come after him seemed to have no bearing on my father's feelings toward me. I had thwarted his vengeance. The hatred he'd felt for me before now came into the open.

Chapter Six

ARRIOLA WAS a brand-new, booming frontier town. Its streets were a sea of deep mud, crusting over now at dusk with frost, but churned up by the unending stream of freight wagons, buggies and buckboards. Boots made a constant thunder on the new boardwalks, and from the half-dozen or more saloons came the discordant tinkle of as many tinny pianos.

A painted woman with an ostrich-feather hat smiled and called out something to me as I drove down the street. My face flamed red and I looked away, wondering at the excitement that mingled with fright inside me.

I pulled up before the rude, unpainted hotel and called to the men on the walk, "Whereabouts could I find the sheriff?"

They peered into the back of the buckboard and at once they clustered around me. "Whatcha got, kid?"

Embarrassed suddenly, I said, " 'Pache."

"Not K Diamond's 'Pache?" The fame of K Diamond's Apache scourge had apparently traveled far.

I nodded.

"You took 'im alive?"

I was beginning to feel real good because of their admiring stares. One of them said, "He's Rob King's kid, by hell." Another said, "Just let me climb up there with you, buster. I'll take you to the sheriff."

If it hadn't been for knowing what I faced at home, that would have been one of the finest moments of my life. I was Rob King's kid, and for the moment at least, just like him—just as good as he was. I drove, and the man beside me, a bearded, jovial fellow, directed me. We drove down the street with the growing crowd plodding along through the mud behind us.

They noticed my knife-ripped sheepskin, and the slashed place in my boot, and commented admiringly on it, not once taking notice that the Indian was skinny and half-starved and weak because of it.

The jail was a new adobe building with thick steel bars at its windows. I pulled up in front and got down from the buckboard seat, and a couple of the men went in to get the sheriff, a young, dark-haired man whose manner plainly showed his sense of new-found importance. He ordered a couple of the men to carry the Indian in, and they dumped him in the single cell and slashed his bonds. He jumped up, of course, and tried to get away, but his legs failed him, having been tied up so long. He fell down and the men scurried out, slamming the barred door.

"What's the charge, son?" the sheriff asked me.

I didn't like that "son." I said, "Killin' K Diamond cattle, I reckon."

The sheriff pursed his lips importantly. "Wanton destruction of private property. That cover it?"

"Reckon it does."

"This here's an Injun. I 'spect you know that means he can't be treated like an ordinary criminal. We got to notify the military authorities over to Fort Meade we got him. Then we'll see what happens."

I believe until then I hadn't quite realized the enormity of the thing I'd done. Now, suddenly, I did. The Apache had an HT branded on his rump. The military was going to want to know how it got there. Pa was in trouble. I wished frantically that I could somehow undo what I had done.

I was tired of the sheriff all at once, tired of his self-importance and posing. I went out and drove over to Meier's Mercantile. I gave gruff old Hans Meier the list Pa'd made and told him to load it all up tonight. I'd stable the horses and buckboard afterward, and would be ready to leave at dawn. Then I went out to wander around town.

It was barely light now, with cold dusk settling rapidly over the busy streets. A big Concord coach came lurching down the street behind spans of galloping horses, and stopped. A woman alighted and minced through the mud to the walk. A couple of important-looking men in gray broadcloth suits and beaver hats escorted her to the hotel, with a stage company roustabout following behind loaded with baggage.

Arriola was as rough a frontier town as you could find,

but that day it seemed like a new world to me.

Even in winter, it was redolent of strange smells, the faint perfume of the woman coach passenger, the sour-warm odor of liquor that characterized the front of each saloon I passed, the decaying smell of a pile of bones beside the makeshift slaughterhouse, and over all the smell of manure from stables and corrals and steaming piles in the muddy street.

And the people were as wildly different as the smells. Filthy, blanketed Indians squatted stolidly and impassively before Meier's Mercantile, waiting for I knew not what. Monstrous, bearded teamsters wheeled their loaded wagons along through the mud amid hoarse shouts and the vicious cracking of their whips. Gamblers with their fancy clothes and glittering stickpins, their soft white hands and smooth-shaven faces, left the saloons and headed for the dining room in the rude hotel. Careful-eyed strangers who looked as wild and untamed as the town lounged on the walks.

I went back to Meier's and bought myself new boots and a new sheepskin. The buckboard was loaded, so I drove it to the livery barn and left it there for the night.

Going back toward the hotel, I looked with mingled longing and fright at each saloon I passed, feeling a return of the vague excitement I'd felt earlier when the woman spoke to me.

I felt almost a man that night in town, and ready to face Pa and his wrath over what I'd done with the Apache.

Driving out the next morning, I felt altogether different.

The town, the sights and smells and excitement it engendered in me was behind, and K Diamond was ahead.

Chester Wolfe, the new man Pa had kept out of his trail-drive crew, and Manuel set about unloading the buckboard into the lean-to behind the house. Pa and I went inside.

Suddenly I was scared. I said, "Pa, I caught the Apache."

Instantly Pa's eyes flared, and a strange tension came into his huge frame. "Where's his body? I'll send Manuel after it right away."

His eyes showed a pride in me I'd never seen there before. I said, trying not to sound defensive, "He ain't dead. I hauled him in to Arriola and turned him over to the sheriff."

Pa froze. The color drained out of his face and for an endless moment he was like a carved stone statue. His voice came out, shocked and unbelieving. "You mean after all he's done to us you done that? You mean after all the days and weeks of hopeless trailin'—" He stopped and stared at me. He made no effort to conceal his bitter disappointment.

Being scared, and, as usual, unable to measure up to him, I retreated into sullenness. Pa stamped out of the house with the parting words, "I suppose you knew what would happen when the military found that brand on him?"

I didn't answer. Nothing I could have said would have changed anything.

He was gone until late that night, riding, I suppose,

trying to think it out. And I know he came to the conclusion that night that it wasn't enough to hold K Diamond by force. He had to spread out, to control the law and the courts as well.

I was in bed when he returned. I wasn't asleep, but I pretended to be, and listened to him talking to Manuel.

He said, "I'm going to Arriola tomorrow, Manuel. I'll take Jeff with me. I'm goin' to send him up to Denver to school. He's damn nigh sixteen now."

So this was to be my punishment for turning the Apache over to the law. Pa seemed to be thinking out loud. "I'll send you back some men. Could be we'll need 'em before this business about that 'Pache is finished."

That was the night K Diamond grew up, changing from an outfit that was held together with spit and determination, to one that was held together by half a score of men and a lot of invisible tentacles that eventually reached all the way to Denver and the territorial legislature.

And although I didn't know it then, that was the night Pa made up his mind to bring a woman back to K Diamond with him. He had decided that I was too soft to ever succeed in holding K Diamond together after he was gone.

He wanted another son and he went about getting a mother for that son in much the same cold-blooded way he'd go about finding a suitable mare for the blooded Kentucky stallion he'd recently had brought all the way from Louisville.

I believe it was that night I really began to return his hate.

I suppose in every father-son relationship there is some hatred. There is also love, and sometimes a kind of desperate longing for affection and approval. . . .

I know that I tried hard to understand my father during the next few years. But I failed, and in failing knew a bitter frustration that fed my hatred until there were times when it filled my life.

I went up to Denver by stagecoach and rail in midwinter, and arrived in time to begin the spring term. My schooling had been long neglected, and for a while there was some difficulty about getting me into a proper grade. But I worked hard, perhaps to escape the confused thoughts of home and K Diamond, and by summer was placed in the eighth grade.

I stayed in Denver all summer, working under a private tutor, and in the fall, took a place in school rightful for my age.

When I returned home that winter for the Christmas holidays, I scarcely knew K Diamond. There was a big new bunkhouse to house the fifteen-man crew. The house had been enlarged to more than three times its former size. And I had a new half-brother, a tiny, wizened, red-faced mite, whose mother, pallid and hollow-eyed, I didn't even recognize as the woman who had smiled and spoken to me on the street of Arriola that day I'd driven into town with the Apache tied up in the wagon.

Her influence was visible throughout the house, in the deep-piled red carpets that covered the new hardwood floors, in the rococo vases and knickknacks that littered the top of every table in sight, in the velvet draperies that hung at the windows. She'd effectively converted the K Diamond into a kind of plush parlor house, probably without even realizing what she was doing.

At first I was stiff and embarrassed in her presence. Gradually, however, I got to know her, and to like her.

Her name was Annie. She was a pretty thing perhaps five years my senior. She had a surface hardness that had completely fooled my father, who at first had believed her hardness went all the way to her core. But underneath, I discovered, she was soft, uncertain and afraid.

Perhaps in myself she recognized a kindred spirit, a half-defiant source of disappointment to my father, as she herself was. At any rate, after the first couple of days, we became good friends.

"I hope you won't resent me, Jeff," she told me with touching frankness. "I married your father for reasons that aren't hard to understand. He offered me security for life in exchange for a son. You know what I was before, Jeff. You're seventeen, and a man. But now I'm beginning to be sorry I accepted. When I came here this was practically a shack. I don't suppose I quite realized how rich your father was. Now I'm beginning to see the position I'm supposed to fill, and I know I can't do it. I'll be gone when you come home again, Jeff. I'll stay until my baby's weaned and then I'll go."

I wanted to protest, but my tongue seemed stuck to the roof of my mouth. Her face was almost transparent and her eyes were enormous above the dark circles that pain had caused. They glistened with tears as she talked. She was another of my father's victims. She loved him, but she knew her love was not returned and never would be.

His attitude toward her rather surprised me, however. He treated her with a kind of quiet courtesy that amounted almost to deference. If I had tried harder, or perhaps if I'd been a few years older, I might have understood that he was sorry for the way he'd behaved with her and by his courtesy and deference was trying to right the wrong.

Honor-bound by his own bargain, I know now that he'd have kept her there all of her natural life. If she'd been what he had thought her to be, she'd have stayed, too. But she wasn't, and so when I returned home in June of the following year, I found she had left.

Chapter Seven

PA SEEMED almost to have forgotten me that summer. I came and went as I pleased, with no interference from him except for a casual inquiry once regarding what I was studying in school and what I wanted to be. He no longer seemed concerned about whether or not I intended to make a career of K Diamond. He was putting his hopes on the red-faced toddler whom he had named Lee, and who was now in the care of an elderly Mexican woman.

The work of the ranch went on, the line-riding, digging out water holes, breaking horses, doctoring and corral building. Some days I'd ride out with Manuel, whose hair was showing a little gray now, and some I'd ride by myself, content to let the wild, tangy smell of the open range flow in and out of my lungs, content to let my thoughts wander.

There were times when I'd be too far from the house to return at night, and I'd stay overnight at one of the many tiny line camp cabins that now dotted K Diamond's vast miles of range.

Or I'd visit one or another of our neighbors, sometimes old Martin Longstreet, whose Southern drawl and stories of the old days could hold my interest for hours. But whether I realized it or not, the place I visited most often was old Mrs. Peckham's, over in the cedar hills that bordered the meandering Arriola River.

Her son had been killed in a saloon ruckus in Arriola a year or so before. Now she lived alone with Rose, who had changed from the lanky girl I remembered into a young woman, and a mighty pretty one.

Mrs. Peckham was a strange woman, seeming more man than woman. You seldom saw her in a dress. Usually she wore a pair of baggy linsey-woolsey pants and a man's shirt. Her feet were encased invariably in a pair of scuffed, heeled boots, spurred like a man's, and her legs were slightly bowed from riding. Her face was withered as an apple and she wore her long gray hair piled in a knot atop her head so it would fit under the high crown of her flop-brimmed man's hat.

Although Rose rode as hard and worked the cattle just as her mother did, she dressed like a woman. Perhaps in rebellion against the garb worn by her mother, she dressed in boots, and split riding skirt; and almost always wore, instead of a man's shirt, a kind of Mexican *camisa,* or blouse.

She was a vital, dark-eyed girl, with full, smiling lips and wide, prominent cheekbones. She had a way about her, a lithe way of moving that made me very conscious of her body beneath her clothes. She flaunted herself, and I am not sure it was entirely unconscious. I believe she was attracted to me, as I was to her.

Yet there was never anything between us save for small talk about range and cattle and the sudden growth of Arriola, for we were never together except in the dour presence of the old lady. But always, a current seemed to flow between us, a current that made each moment together an exciting and memorable experience.

I can never forget, nor do I want to, the day in late summer when I got caught in a heavy afternoon thundershower too far away from shelter to protect myself. I just rode it out because there wasn't anything else to do. I was pretty well soaked and beginning to chill from the wind that accompanied the rain, so when I saw smoke from a fire over in the next draw, I naturally headed that way, thinking some cowpuncher had built a fire to dry off.

The cedars were pretty thick on this particular part of our range, which was close to the Arriola River. But it was our range so the last person I expected to see was Rose Peckham.

I came out of the screen of cedars and there stood Rose beside the fire, her inky black hair let out to dry and reaching almost to her waist. She held her blouse in her hands, spread to the fire to dry, and her breasts were bare. She whirled to face me as she heard the sound of my horse, and immediately held the *camisa* against her. But not before I had seen the swelling roundness of breasts and their darktipped nipples.

I know I turned brick-red, and she did too. I stammered something and turned my horse around to give her time to put on her blouse. There was mocking humor in her voice as she said, "All right, Jeff. You can look now."

Her color was still high as I dismounted. I thought there was a certain excitement in her dark eyes, a sort of veiled challenge.

Her hair streamed out, a flood of black silk that engulfed her shoulders and upper arms. I didn't say anything, and I know I was still blushing. She said, smiling and wetting her lips, "Well, don't just stand there. Come on over and dry out. It's what you came for, isn't it?"

I nodded and spread my hands to the blaze. I was shaking. It wasn't from the cold, but from excitement. I'd wanted to be alone with her for a long time.

After a few moments she said, "I'll bet you knew lots of girls up there in Denver."

"Not so many."

"How many?"

"Couple, maybe." I hadn't really known any. I'd just gone to school with some. I tried to keep my eyes from wandering to the places where her breasts thrust against the thin, wet material of her blouse. I tried to keep myself from remembering what they'd looked like, all bare and shining and proud. A fire kindled inside me and grew hotter as I gazed into her eyes.

She moved around the fire, and licked her lips. She was poised like a frightened doe, looking as though she'd like to run but didn't really want to.

Her voice sounded strange as she said, "I'll bet you've kissed lots of girls."

"I haven't either."

"You're just funnin'. I'll bet you know how to kiss a girl the way she wants to be kissed."

"You want to be kissed?"

"Maybe. Why don't you try and see?"

There was a kind of fascination about standing there so close to her, a delicious ecstasy of waiting, of being afraid, of knowing what was going to happen, half afraid that it would, terrified that it wouldn't.

I said, "Maybe I will." But I didn't move.

Her lips were heavy and parted, and her teeth gleamed white between them. There was no smile on her lips or in her eyes. Her breasts rose and fell with her rapid breathing.

"Well, go on then. What you waitin' for?"

I reached for her clumsily. Her arms flew about my neck and her body molded itself against me. Her wet mouth found mine, half open. A light nip with her teeth opened my mouth, and then I felt her tongue, darting, searing. I pulled away, frightened at what was happening to me.

I could still feel the burn of her body along my whole length. Leaving me standing there, she went over and unsaddled her horse. She flung the blanket down on the wet ground. She was pale and her hands were shaking. She sat down on the blanket, looking up at me with an odd inscrutable expression. She said, "Jeff?"

"What?"

"Want to look again?" She was fumbling with the top button of her blouse.

"Maybe."

The blouse came off. She put her hands on the blanket behind her to support her and sat that way, looking up at me with defiant embarrassment. She began to shiver when I didn't move, and at last she whispered, "Jeff, I'm cold."

I walked over to the blanket and sat down beside her. She threw her arms around my neck and pulled me down. My lips found hers and I seemed to be drowning. She took my hand and put it on one of her breasts, and the fire inside me spread, leaped, flared until I thought it would consume me.

We were both awkward, and shy, yet in spite of that there was an overwhelming beauty in the experience, the beauty of a lightning bolt striking a tree. But when it was over the beauty was gone and remaining was only the smoldering gray ash of guilt. As with the tree destroyed by lightning, something had been destroyed, yet not wholly destroyed, for it would remain as the blasted tree remained, a reminder forever.

Both of us found difficulty in meeting each other's eyes. We mumbled our words to each other as I helped her saddle her horse. She seemed as anxious as I to leave, to go her separate way, yet as I rode away I heard a sound behind me, I thought the sound of Rose's crying. Whether she cried from anger or hurt or shame, I didn't know.

For the remainder of the summer I avoided the cedar hills of the Arriola River. I tried to put the incident from my mind, but the harder I tried, the worse I failed. In my mind I kept seeing Rose sitting on that blanket looking at me, her eyes enormous and pleading, yet frightened and half ashamed too. When I'd think of her, the excitement would leap in me until my blood was pounding through my body. My hands would shake. And yet I couldn't go back, for the thing that had happened that day loomed like a wall between us.

Pa could have helped me that summer if I'd been able to confide in him. But he scarcely noticed me. He seemed determined to put me from his mind, the way he'd tried to put me out of his life by sending me north to school. . . .

Manuel was the one who noticed that I'd stopped going over toward the Arriola River. Maybe he noticed that something was bothering me too, and with his wry, earthy insight, guessed what was wrong.

I was sitting one day on the corral wall, idly watching the big sorrel stallion Pa'd brought from Kentucky. I don't suppose Manuel could have known about the rainy afternoon I'd spent with Rose, although I might be wrong about that. But he apparently knew exactly what was the matter with me.

He came to the corral, leading a mare that hadn't got bred in June when she should have.

Immediately the stallion, which we called Jubal, came trotting to the corral gate. He snorted shrilly, his eyes wide and glistening and attentive. He reared and came down prancing. The muscles in his neck stood out. His hide glistened, his great neck arched.

Manuel opened the gate and turned the mare in. Then he climbed up beside me. He said nothing, nor did he look at me after that first searching glance.

The mare laid back her ears and nipped at the stallion. She reared and kicked at him. He avoided her hoofs nimbly and bit her on the rump. She squealed and began to run around the corral.

He headed her off and bit her withers. Again she laid her ears back and whirled to kick. But this time she didn't kick. She just stood there, trembling.

I sat very still, staring with fascination. I'd seen cows bred, but never before a mare. There was grace and beauty in the stallion's movement, a purely male power and domination that made me catch my breath.

When it was finished, the stallion stood in the center of the corral, spent, exhausted, his hide gleaming and velvety with sweat, and the mare trotted to the gate as though nothing had happened and waited to be let out.

Manuel made no move to open the gate. I felt that he was watching me, and I was suddenly embarrassed. His voice, when he spoke, was unbelievably soft, "This is a thing, Señor Jeff, which only man defiles with shame. Animals are wiser. They do not question God, or try to make something unclean out of something so clean and beautiful."

He didn't wait for me to answer. He slipped down off the corral fence and opened the gate. He led the mare away and after a few moments I turned my head and saw him riding out.

Chapter Eight

I WENT BACK to school in the fall. I'd decided to become a lawyer, and for once, surprisingly, father seemed to approve. I know he was counting on little Lee to grow up hard enough to hold K Diamond together, but other developments had convinced him that in these changing times a knowledge of the law might be useful too.

K Diamond had become an obsession with him. His earlier determination to look after his own had not lessened, but the ranch itself now had its hold on him.

When I returned to K Diamond in June of the following year, now eighteen, I found little Lee enormously grown, a sturdy, smiling fellow with a round, cheerful face and an engaging manner that announced he liked the world and everything in it.

Again I noticed how K Diamond had grown. There were half a dozen new buildings, including an enormous barn and a galleried series of horse stalls almost a hundred feet long. It was beginning to look like a town in itself, dominated as always by the sprawling, added-to ranch house which had begun so simply with a single, adobe shack.

Father seemed unchanged, save for a sprinkling of gray in his tawny hair and mustache. I didn't think he looked a day older than when we came here, but I suppose change is so gradual that one doesn't notice it. And yet I expected change in him, probably because I was changing so rapidly myself? I realized suddenly that he was only in his late thirties.

I could tell, even as I drew the livery stable buggy to a halt before the house that something was wrong. Manuel was out in the corral saddling a pair of horses. He looked up, saw me, and started toward me. Then he took a look at my father, who was just coming out of the house, and went on with his work.

Pa was belting his gun around his middle. His face wore a look of angry concentration, and his movements were hurried. He seemed annoyed at the interruption of my arrival.

I climbed down and he stuck out his hand. "Jeff! Good to see you. Lordy, you've spread out, ain't you?" He grinned briefly as I clasped his hand.

I asked, "How's little Lee? How're Manuel and Chester Wolfe and the others?"

"Fine. Go on in and see your brother. I'll see you later."

I knew this look about him. Chester Wolfe came riding in at this instant and started toward me, a pleased grin crinkling his narrow face, but Pa said sharply, "Get your saddle on a fresh horse, Ches. We've got a little job to do."

Suddenly I couldn't bear to see the three of them ride out at the very instant of my homecoming. I yanked my valise out of the buggy and said, "Put the buggy horse in the corral for me, Pa. I'll be with you in two minutes."

Wherever they were going, I was going too. Behind me as I went along the gallery toward the door I heard Pa say, "Jeff, you wait. We'll be back—" But I was already inside.

I went at once to my room. I found my old riding

clothes in the closet exactly as I'd left them, and changed as quickly as I could. Not knowing why, I strapped on the Dance Brothers and Park revolver without bothering to check the loads. The powder flask still hung from the belt, as did the bullet pouch and the smaller pouch of caps. If the gun needed reloading, I'd do it as I rode.

Outside, the three were just mounting up. Manuel had caught and saddled a horse for me, and I grabbed its reins and mounted.

At a canter, the four of us went west toward the badlands. Manuel dropped back beside me at once, and reined over until our legs touched. His face wrinkled into a thousand tiny lines of humor and welcome, and his teeth flashed white. His black eyes were sparkling beads as he stuck out his thin, powerful hand. "Señor Jeff. Ah, Dios, you are a big man now."

I took his hand, a warm feeling spreading through me. I asked, "What's up, Manuel? Why all the rush?"

He shrugged expressively. "Cattle thieves. They pick at us from all sides. They do not take many. Never more than half a dozen in any one bunch. I picked up fresh sign early this morning. Two men and four head of cattle, driving into the badlands. We go to catch them if we can."

I couldn't help thinking of the time the three Mexicans had trailed their cattle to K Diamond, and had braced father and Manuel in the yard over the theft. The three who now lay buried near the house.

Manuel, with his uncanny insight, guessed my thoughts, for he murmured, "The shoe is on the other foot now, Señor Jeff. And we do what those three tried to do so long ago."

I said, "There's a sheriff in Arriola, isn't there? Why doesn't Pa go to him?"

Manuel glanced at Pa, riding with Chester Wolfe fifty feet ahead, then back at me. "You know the answer to that, Jeff. Arriola is fifty miles away. A day going, and a day coming back. You think we could catch these thieves two days from now?"

I was beginning to wish I hadn't come. I also found myself hoping Pa wouldn't catch up with the thieves.

I think I knew what Pa intended to do when he caught them. The certainty of it sickened me. No trial. Only a pair of ropes thrown over the nearest tree, and two dangling forms, their heads twisted at a grotesque angle.

Manuel must have guessed my thoughts. He said, "Go back, Jeff. Go back and wait for us."

But I shook my head. With the idealism of my eighteen years I felt it was time someone stopped Pa from playing God on K Diamond. I was going to be a lawyer, and I couldn't countenance breaking the law or letting Pa take it into his own hands. I was going along to see to it the rustlers were taken into Arriola and held for trial.

I felt mighty big, riding along, knowing what I was going to do. The old days were gone. Law had come to the territory and it was time to respect it. I fancied myself in the role of its defender on K Diamond.

Canter and trot. Walk and trot. Pa rode ahead, his arm hanging straight down, cavalry fashion, his thumb touching the skirt of his saddle. Reins in the left hand, a ramrod in his back.

My mind conjured up situations which might arise, and of which I was always the master. Pa facing me, a rope coiled in his hand. Myself standing straight and strong, looking him in the eye and saying, "No. They're going to Arriola for trial."

The rustlers looking at me with fearful respect. Manuel breathing softly, "Dios! He is a man, Señor Rob." And then respect coming into Pa's eyes for the first time, his hand extending for a firm clasp of friendship.

I went on from there: brilliant defense attorney in the Territorial capital, and recognition from the Governor. Then County prosecutor, with the world at my feet. If an eagle can fly, let him fly high. Senator from the new state of Colorado. Anything was possible in my mind that day, all of it made so by my fearless defense of a pair of two-bit rustlers.

We traveled hard and we traveled fast. In late afternoon Manuel moved ahead, and shortly thereafter picked up the rustlers' trail. Four head of cattle, by their tracks three-year-olds and probably steers. Two riders, driving them hard and fast.

Fear had set the rustlers' pace. Fear of K Diamond, and of Rob King. I didn't realize it at the time, nor would I have admitted it if I had, but if K Diamond had been protected only by the sheriff in Arriola, the rustlers' fear would have been nonexistent—and instead of driving four, they'd have been driving forty.

We swept along in their trail, now at a steady canter, squeezing together the remaining hours of daylight. Into the badlands we went, a maze of bare hills, of twisting valleys through which wound deep, dry washes, of an occasional spring or seep surrounded by scrubby cotton-woods. And at dusk we came into sight of the Anson brothers' place, with the tracks leading in openly, without fear or subterfuge. That was Rob King's luck, coupled with our speed in following the trail. There were four fat steers down in Anson's corral.

By morning the steers would have been gone, the tracks explainable by the words, "Found four of our strays on your range, Rob. Brought 'em home."

Only now it was different—four K Diamond steers in Anson's corral. We paused at the crest of the rise for an instant, grouping, and then, without a signal from Pa, swarmed down the slight incline toward the rude shack at its bottom.

To this day every detail of that scene is drawn indelibly on my memory. The cabin was flat-roofed adobe, so small you wondered how three men could crowd them-selves into it, with poles sticking far enough out in front to make a narrow gallery. The yard in front of the house was whitened with soapsuds. There was another adobe building, its roof falling in, and a small, eight-sided corral with poles for a gate.

A hog rooted idly at an overturned dishpan on the ground. A dirty white chicken flew from the ground to roost on the caved-in roof of the barn. The awful bare-ness was everywhere.

Rolie Anson, shirtless, in his yellowed long underwear, sprinted frantically for the corral and tried to get the pole gate down to let the cattle out. Clay, his brother, stood in the doorway holding a rifle, and was afraid to use it.

Manuel, without slowing his horse, galloped to the corral to stop Rolie. And Rolie, in panic, drew and fired his gun with an unexpectedness that took us all by surprise.

At the sound of the shot, Pa bellowed at Clay, "Drop it, you son of a bitch!"

Clay dropped it. It clattered at his feet. I looked over toward the corral. Manuel had dismounted and was doubled over, holding his belly. Rolie stared at him wildly for an instant, then threw his gun away with a kind of frightened revulsion. He whirled and began to run.

Wolfe, still mounted, rode after him, taking down his rope. The loop settled neatly over Rolie's head. He managed to get his hands under it between the rope and his neck before it tightened. He jerked and flopped to the ground, kicking like a beheaded chicken.

Wolfe let him get to his feet, then rode back to where we stood, with Rolie trotting behind trying to keep enough slack in the rope. Manuel turned and walked toward us, pain contorting his face, his hands still clutching his belly. Red leaked from between his fingers, and he walked in jerky, uncertain steps.

Pa yelled, "Get in the house, Ches. Get the third one."

Chester Wolfe swung off his horse, his rope still dallied to the horn. With gun in hand, and crouching a little, he ran into the adobe shack. I heard him yelling, his words indistinguishable, and then he came out. "Other one ain't here, Rob."

Pa looked at me for the first time. "Go in the house and

light a lamp."

I swung down, numb, and rushed into the house. I was shaking so badly I could hardly light the lamp even after I'd found it. I kept thinking of Manuel, shot in the belly, his life leaking out between his fingers.

I heard Pa say, "Watch 'em Ches," and he came into the house, helping Manuel to the filthy, rumpled bed. Manuel lay down with a weak groan. I stared with dumb shock, while Pa gently unfastened the front of Manuel's shirt and looked at the wound.

Manuel made a small grin that brought a choking lump to my throat. "The finish. *Es verdad?*"

Pa growled, "Hell, no. Don't be a damned fool." He took a clean bandanna from his pocket and folded it into a compress. He put the compress on the wound and put Manuel's hand over it.

Rooted to the dirt floor, I stared at Manuel. Every one of the thousand kindnesses he'd shown me came flooding back; every one of the golden moments I'd spent with him learning the way of the desert. Suddenly I began to tremble violently. I'd seen death before, but never before had it touched me like this.

Manuel was growing paler. His face seemed almost gray in the flickering lamplight. Pa looked at me and looked quickly away. I knew why Pa did nothing.

Manuel turned his head with difficulty and looked at me. He whispered, "Señor Jeff."

I went over to the side of the bed. His face crinkled into a thousand lines of humor and his mouth tipped up into the old, irrepressible grin. I could see in his eyes that he wished to tell me something. But death was too close. His eyes closed and his grin faded. He was dead.

I think I know what he wanted to tell me, that a strong, ruthless hand had been needed to build K Diamond; that I should try to understand my father instead of condemning him.

I could feel Pa tightening beside me. I could feel the emanation of hatred, and anger, and grief; and I knew that now he would exact his vengeance.

I looked down at Manuel, as though seeking to draw strength from him. My father rushed out, and I turned and ran after him.

Chapter Nine

IT WAS NOT QUITE DARK in the yard. You could still see the horizon, the deep gray of the sky hovering above like a cloud. My nerves were jumping within my arms and legs, but I was no longer trembling. Chester Wolfe stood with a gun dangling negligently from his hand, watching the two Ansons who stood together, talking in low, frightened tones. The rope still connected Rolie Anson's neck to Chester Wolfe's saddlehorn, but Rolie was apparently scared to take it off.

You could tell instantly that they were brothers. Both were tall and a little stooped, and appeared to be near thirty. They had straw-colored hair that was straight and coarse, and which didn't appear to have been combed at all. Clay's was plastered against his forehead and you could see a damp depression circling his head where his hat had been. Neither of them was shaven, but they didn't have beards, only a crop of straw-colored whiskers maybe a week old.

Clay cleared his throat as Pa stepped out. "This is the first time we've touched your stock, Rob. I swear to God. We'll make it good. We'll pay you good an' give you the four steers back too."

Pa didn't say anything. He just stared at Rolie, his eyes as cold as ice. Pa looked at Clay then and finally asked, "How much will you pay for Manuel?"

Clay swallowed. He tried to meet Pa's stare and couldn't. He looked at Chester Wolfe and finally at me. He babbled in a hoarse, whisper, "Don't let him do it, Jeff."

I turned my head and looked at Pa. Clay probably thought I was refusing him, for he swung on Chester Wolfe. "Ches, don't—"

Pa's voice cut in, sharp as razor steel. "Get the saddle off my horse, Ches. That cottonwood down by the spring will do."

Wolfe began to unsaddle Pa's horse. I wanted to say something but I didn't know what to say. Numb and silent, I watched. When Ches had flung Pa's saddle to the ground, Pa said, "You're first, Rolie. Climb up."

Rolie fell to the ground. He was blubbering like a kid. "Please! Oh God, Rob, don't! Manuel had a gun in his hand. I thought he was goin' to shoot."

Pa's voice was implacable. "You snivelin' bastard, get on my horse!"

Rolie crawled toward Pa, begging. I felt my stomach

rising in my throat. When Rolie was near enough, Pa kicked him. "Get up."

Rolie rolled, hugging his belly. Pa kicked him again, angrily. "Damn you, get up!"

Clay's voice interrupted, "Take me first, Rob." Without waiting for Pa's reply, he walked over and vaulted to the bare back of Pa's horse. Chester Wolfe was fashioning a hangman's noose in the end of Pa's rope. When he had it finished, he handed it up to Clay. Clay hesitated then he put it around his neck and adjusted it so that the heavy part of the knot was on one side.

His eyes, so pale and gray, had a staring quality to them that will haunt me to the end of my days. I shuddered and found my tongue. I said, "Pa, you can't do this!"

"Who the hell says I can't?" He swung on me, his eyes blazing.

The courage I fancied I'd have while riding here didn't exist at all. I was almost as scared as Clay Anson, as though it were I Pa was going to hang, and not the Ansons. My voice didn't sound like my own, but thank God it was steady. "Take 'em in to Arriola. Let the law hang them. Give 'em a fair trial."

Pa laughed contemptuously. "Did they give Manuel one? Anyhow what the hell will a trial prove that ain't already proved? There's the cattle over there in the corral. Go look at 'em if you want. I saw the K Diamond on 'em when I rode in. Go take a look at Manuel."

"But—"

"You were with us. You trailed those four head of K Diamond steers right along with us. And the trail led here. You saw that snivelin' son shoot Manuel. You saw Manuel die. What the hell's a trial for, anyway?"

"To find out whether they're guilty or not."

"You reckon there's any doubt?"

I shook my head, remembering the concepts of American law. I felt foolish but stubborn as I said, "The law says a man's innocent until he's proved guilty. It says man's entitled to a trial by jury. The law's to protect the people, so there won't be any mistakes made. It's to protect you just as much as it's to protect these two."

Pa was trying to be fair, but I could see he thought me only a stubborn, damned-fool kid, spouting off the smattering of knowledge I'd only half learned.

He asked bitterly, "Did the law protect your ma? Did it protect us from that stock-killin' Apache? Did it protect us against the likes of these two?"

The words were on my tongue, "Manuel would still be alive if you'd gone to the law about this," but I didn't say them because I realized it would be unfair. I kept remembering the way Manuel had looked at me, the way he'd tried to speak to me as he died. I was thinking back to our beginnings here, when there was no law closer than three hundred miles; if a man wanted to live through those times he'd had to make his own law. Perhaps the time for it was passing, but it was not yet past. That was what Manuel had tried to tell me—that I was of one generation, my father another.

Pa seemed to forget me. He led the horse over beneath the cottonwood, holding the reins in one hand, the noose rope with the other. Chester Wolfe yanked Rolie to his feet and followed.

Pa threw the rope over the cottonwood limb and tied it around the trunk, first drawing it snug. His words seemed to come from a distance, "You got anything to say, Clay?"

"Yeah. You're a dirty bastard."

Pa quirted the horse's rump. And an instant later, Clay hit the end of the rope.

His head flopped over to one side. He made a choking, gagging sound. Then, kicking weakly, he swung back and forth, his feet but inches from the ground.

Sweating, I watched while they hoisted Rolie to the horse's back. Rolie was babbling with fear, and struggling. They got another noose around his neck and over the cottonwood limb, and after that he quit trying to dive off the horse. Pa said, "Anything to say, Rolie?"

"Yeah. Please, Rob, please. For God's sake—" He broke off and began to whimper. Pa quirted the horse for a second time.

Leaving the two there, swinging grotesquely, Pa and Chester Wolfe came back to where I stood, leading their horses and Manuel's too. Pa didn't look at me, but Chester Wolfe did. Ches's face was gray and his hands were shaking.

Pa went into the shack and came out, carrying Manuel's body in his arms the way a woman carries a child. He laid Manuel over his saddle, hooking Manuel's belt over the horn to hold him in place. He seemed to be talking to himself as he said, "He ought to have a buckboard to ride in. But I'm afraid of what Dell Anson might do when he gets back."

We rode away, Pa leading Manuel's horse, Ches following, and I brought up the rear. . . .

Chapter Ten

WE WERE OUT on the slope behind the house in the scorching sun burying Manuel when Dell Anson rode in.

Pa had sent to Arriola during the night for a priest, since Manuel had been of the Catholic faith and would have wanted one. It was past noon when the priest arrived in the K Diamond buggy driven by Chester Wolfe, the new foreman of K Diamond.

Out of deference to me, perhaps, Pa had also sent for the sheriff, Roscoe Brady, and Brady had ridden out early on horseback.

One of K Diamond's crewmen, who had once been a carpenter, had made a coffin during the night. We were lowering it awkwardly into the ground by means of rope slings when we heard the hurried drum of hoofs. Looking up I saw Dell Anson pounding toward us.

I had a hold on little Lee's pudgy hand. He was whimpering and tugging against me, trying to get loose so he could play in the fresh dirt that had been taken out of the grave.

I think everyone there figured Dell was riding to sure death, and I have an idea Dell figured that too. He was nearly out of his mind with grief and shock and probably past caring. He'd come home and found his two brothers swinging from the cottonwood. He'd taken time to bury them, probably, and then had come for his revenge.

I thought Dell looked more like Clay than Rolie. Dell was the oldest by a year or so, but he kept himself better than his brothers had. He was nearly always clean-shaven, and he had a more friendly manner. I doubt if he was involved in rustling K Diamond stock, although he could hardly have failed to know that his brothers were.

Our crew looked at Pa, waiting for their cue. They were all armed and could have cut Dell down easily. But Pa shook his head.

Dell pulled his lathered horse to a halt. His eyes, pale gray like those of his brothers, were wild. He glared at Pa, breathing hard as though he had run all the way here instead of the horse.

Roscoe Brady stepped toward Dell, hat in hand. His face was a little flushed, his eyes uncertain. He said, "No trouble now, Dell. We're burying Manuel Ferrera. Your brother Rolie killed him last night."

Dell didn't even look at Brady. He kept his piercing, accusing stare on Pa. He said slowly, distinctly, "Rob, you murderin' bastard!"

Brady paled. He must have known why Dell had come, but the quiet virulence in Dell's voice likely made his blood chill just as it did mine.

Brady said, "Go on home, Dell. I'll take care of this."

Dell laughed harshly and asked, "What'll you do, Sheriff?"

"I'll hold King for trial by the circuit judge."

Dell looked at him sourly. "You'll hold him in jail?"

"Well—"

"I thought so."

"Dell, damn it, I can't throw a man like Rob King in jail. The judge ain't due for damn near three months. But you've got my word. Rob'll stand trial."

Dell snorted contemptuously, "Hell, I can tell you now what the verdict will be. There ain't a jury in Arriola County that'll convict Rob King, especially since Manuel was killed."

"If he's guilty they'll convict him."

"If he's guilty!" Dell was silent for a moment, trembling. He was still hovering on the raw edge of violence, but all this talk had slowed him down. He looked around at the K Diamond crew; every one had a hand conspicuously near his gun. Dell looked back at Pa. He said, "If you're acquitted I'm going to kill you."

Pa looked at him steadily. "Now's all right, Dell. Right now's fine."

"Sure. It is for you, ain't it? You've only got fifteen guns to back you up."

Pa looked around. "Boys, don't interfere. If Dell kills me, he's to ride out of here without bein' bothered. Understand?"

Little Lee began to cry beside me. I knelt and put an arm around him to quiet him.

Reluctant K Diamond hands slid away from smooth gun grips. Pa stepped out to be clear of the crewmen near him. He said softly, "All right, Dell."

The priest spoke up, his voice shocked, "Stop it, all of you. A man is dead. We have not yet finished committing his remains to the grave. This is no time for shooting."

Nobody seemed to have heard him. Dell Anson sat his fidgeting horse and Pa waited quietly, showing no more concern than he would talking over a calf crop with Ches.

Dell scowled, but his recklessness was gone under the pressure of Pa's steady unconcern. He said, "I ain't givin' up. If they let you go I'll get you myself." He wheeled his horse and rode away as furiously as he had ridden in.

We all watched him until he was out of sight. When I looked at Pa he seemed to have forgotten Dell Anson. He stood gravely waiting for the services to resume. There was more sadness in his face than I had seen there since the night of mother's death, and I realized just how much Manuel had meant to Pa.

The priest finished the services and the crew dispersed, silent and subdued. Pa went into the house with Sheriff Brady, and Ches drove away in the buggy with the priest. I sat down on the porch steps, keeping one eye on Lee, who was tumbling around on the ground with a good-natured old shepherd dog.

Behind me, inside the house, I could hear the drone of Pa's and Brady's voices, their words clearly distinguishable in the quietness.

Brady was saying, "Damn it, I've got to do it, Mr. King. I'll have to remand you for trial. What the hell did you do it for, anyhow? Why didn't you bring 'em in to me? They'd have got hung anyway. Maybe not on the rustlin' charge, but sure as hell on that murder charge."

Pa said intolerantly, "I wanted 'em hanged for the rustlin'."

"Why? Why, for God's sake?"

"So maybe the next bastard that thinks about stealin' K Diamond cattle will think twice."

Brady's voice was angry. "You leave law enforcement to me. I got a mind to hold you in jail."

"Quit dreamin', Brady. You're not holdin' me for anything. And you're not bringin' me to trial."

Brady sputtered. Pa said evenly, "Elections are comin' up in November, ain't they?"

"Yeah. Sure they are. What's that got to do with it?"

"You want to be sheriff again?"

"I do. And I will."

"Maybe. Maybe not: It takes money to run a campaign. You got plenty?"

"What are you getting at, Mr. King?" There was a sort of mild outrage in Brady's voice.

"Just this. Go along with me and you get five thousand for campaign expenses."

"And if I don't?"

"Somebody else gets it—somebody who will play along with K Diamond. You're no fool, Brady, for all your damn pompousness. You know as well as I do that five thousand will tip the election to whoever has that much to spend."

I'd like to have heard Brady's reply. But little Lee commenced to squeal with delight over the dog's attempt to lick his face.

A few minutes later, Brady and Pa came out onto the porch. They shook hands, apparently in agreement. The last words Brady said were, "Don't worry, Rob. Don't worry."

I heard Pa murmur, "Who's worryin'?" but I don't think Brady heard. He went across the yard, got his horse and rode away toward town.

Pa turned to me and grinned. "Times are changin', Jeff. You go on back to school and get to be a good lawyer. You can—"

I interrupted, "You don't need a lawyer. Your gun and your money have done all right so far. If you can't make the law, you buy it." I discovered that I was trembling. I tried to stand up to him, glaring, but the amused, tolerant expression that came to his eyes defeated me. I turned and ran to the corral. I got my horse and rode out, and I didn't come back for two days.

I'd get to be a lawyer, all right. Just as fast I could. But I wouldn't be K Diamond's bought-and-paid-for lawyer. Pa wouldn't buy me as easily as he'd bought Brady.

Somehow, legal justice had to be brought to Arriola County. I figured, in my youthful optimism, that I was just the man who could do the job.

I stayed pretty much away from home until it was time for me to go back to school. And I stopped coming home summers, instead staying in Denver under private tutors so I'd get through sooner.

Three years later I passed the bar, and with my certificate in my pocket, boarded the train for Arriola.

Chapter Eleven

THE TRAIN CHUGGED into the new, yellow frame railroad station at Arriola and stopped. Escaping steam made a deafening racket. I gathered my luggage together and stepped down, at once conscious of my clothes, which had seemed so ordinary in Denver, but which made me self-conscious here.

It was early morning, but already there was a still, oppressive heat to the air. Dust was three inches deep in the street beside the station. It dripped from the wheels of passing freight wagons like water, and raised in a cloud behind each one. Farther up the street a tiny whirlwind raised a solid column of it into the air to a height of fifty feet.

I'd noticed the range as the train neared Arriola, and had wondered why Pa or Ches hadn't mentioned the drouth in their infrequent letters. Perhaps, I decided, it was because K Diamond wasn't hurt from it yet. Or perhaps they simply decided I wouldn't be interested.

I hadn't written to tell them I was arriving, so no one was at the station to meet me. I hadn't wanted to be rushed out to K Diamond. I wanted time to look around town, maybe rent an office, and start practicing.

I laid my bags in a buckboard and climbed to the seat. The driver clucked to the horse and drove up the street toward the hotel.

There was a K Diamond wagon before Meier's Mercantile, loading, of all things, barbed wire. Times were certainly changing, I thought. There'd been a time when Rob King wouldn't have considered the use of wire on his far-flung range.

The buckboard pulled up before the hotel. I got down and looked around while the drayman unloaded my bags and carried them into the lobby. The hotel had a new coat of cedar shakes over its weathered sides, painted brown, and sported a gilt sign over the entrance.

Main Street extended into the prairie a couple of blocks farther than I remembered and it was lined with new, false-fronted store buildings. Off Main I could see clusters of new residences, and could hear the sound of hammers and saws in the distance.

Even this early, the street was busy with horsemen, buckboards, buggies, and heavy freight wagons. The train whistled mournfully as it pulled away from the station, and horses tied at the hotel hitchrail laid back their ears, rolled their eyes and fidgeted at the unaccustomed noise.

A rickety wagon with a canvas top pulled up before Meier's Mercantile down the street and disgorged a ragged farmer, his scrawny wife and a large number of thin, ragged children.

"Lord," I thought. "Homesteaders. Wait till Pa sees them."

The town looked busy and healthy; I was encouraged. There ought to be a place in a town this size for a lawyer, even a lawyer fresh out of law school with a certificate upon which the ink was hardly dry.

I went inside and engaged a room, surprised that I recognized no one I saw. Arriola had become a town of strangers, lately come, I guessed, because of its growth and new prosperity. There were cattle pens down by the tracks, and the land was settled for a hundred miles around.

I cleaned up and shaved, and then went downstairs to stroll around and find an office.

I'd grown and put on weight since leaving K Diamond. I was six feet one that year, same as I am now. I weighed a hundred and seventy-five. Up in Denver I'd tried growing a mustache like Pa's, but had failed at that just as I had failed every other time I'd tried to do something he did. Now I kept my face clean-shaven. My hair was long, in the fashion of the times, and I wore burnsides that reached halfway across my cheeks.

I found an office a block from the hotel and around the corner off Main, and paid fifteen dollars for the first month's rent out of my dwindling store of K Diamond money, which I'd sworn to myself would be the last I ever took from Pa.

My books were delivered later in the day by the station buckboard, and I had a sign painted and hung before nightfall. Next morning I looked up to see my first client entering the door.

Old as I was, and mature as I thought I was, I couldn't help the quick flush that stained my cheeks, for my client was Rose Peckham.

She seemed older than I remembered her, and thinner. But time had not hurt her loveliness. She looked at me, colored prettily and said softly, extending her hand, "Jeff, I'm so glad to see you back."

I took her hand. I realized, perhaps for the first time that day, what an unutterable fool I'd been these past few years. Rose seemed to be having difficulty meeting my eyes, and I knew the memory of what had been between us was in her mind as well as in mine.

Her hand was calloused and rough from work, but nonetheless I held it until Rose began to grow uncomfortable. The old excitement stirred in me and I wanted to take her in my arms, an impulse I fought down. She held up a hand to show me the plain gold band on the third finger of her left hand.

I don't know why it should have hit me so hard. I stammered, "You're married?"

She was kind enough to ignore the things my surprise implied. She said, "Yes, I'm married. To Dell Anson. And it's about Dell that I wanted to see you, Jeff."

I hadn't talked to Rose since that day beside her fire in the cedars. I was ashamed of that, and my shame stood between us like a wall.

I said, "Is Dell in trouble?"

I'd never asked Pa about Dell. But I'd asked Ches in my letters and he'd told me that Dell had apparently decided not to do anything about his brothers' death or about the sheriff's failure to bring Pa to trial. Yet if Dell were in trouble now, it was probably trouble with K Diamond.

I knew I ought to shy off. I'd be a fool if I let my first case be one against my own father. But I knew that I'd do whatever Rose asked me to do.

Rose was still standing, nervously twisting her hands together. I remembered my manners and got her a chair. She settled into it and began to smooth her skirt. "I—I don't know whether—I mean, you're Jeff King. Maybe you wouldn't take a case against K Diamond. I guess I was foolish for coming here."

She was changed. I remembered her as an untamed sort of girl, with a shy boldness about her. Now she was only shy.

Knowing quite well what a fool I was likely to make of myself, I said pompously, "I'm my own man now, Rose. There's no connection between K Diamond and myself that would stop me. I'll take a case against K Diamond as quickly as I'd take any other case."

"Dell won't like my coming to you. But Jennings Bruce is the only other lawyer in town and he's representing your father."

"You don't think my opposing Father will make him harder on Dell than he might be otherwise?"

She laughed bitterly, as though to say he'd already done all he could.

I asked, "What's it all about, Rose?"

Her face was tense, pale. It was a lovely face, made more so by the wide-set, prominent cheekbones, by the hollows beneath them, by her full, red lips. I made myself look away.

"I don't know how much you've heard about the drouth, Jeff. It hasn't hit K Diamond or any of the others too hard yet. Ma has the river and your father has his water holes that never seem to go dry and Sand Creek on the south. Longstreet's up on the mesa and doesn't need to worry much about water. But it's hit us, and Jim Purser over in the badlands pretty hard. Our cattle are dying."

I murmured that was too bad, and waited for her to go on.

"You know about the hatred between Dell and your father. By the time Dell found out your father wasn't going to be tried for hanging his brothers, he was seeing me." There seemed to be a veiled apology in her tone, though I didn't see why she felt she should apologize for anything. If there was blame attached to anyone for what had happened in the cedars, it attached to me, for I realized now that Rose had not given herself wantonly that day.

I remembered the way she used to watch me when I'd visit over at Peckhams, the way she'd seemed to flaunt herself whenever I was around. I'd been blind for not seeing that she was in love with me. And I'd hurt her unforgivably by my avoidance of her.

She was saying, "I talked him out of doing anything rash. I made him see that he couldn't help losing if he went after your father. For one thing, he could never have killed your father unless he did it from ambush. And Dell isn't that kind."

She flushed slightly. "Dell was in love with me even then or he'd never have agreed. But he did agree and he respected his promise."

Perhaps I looked a little puzzled at what she was leading up to. She said, "I'm coming to the trouble." She glanced at me as though wondering how much criticism of my father I would listen to, then squared her shoulders and went on, "Your father persecuted Dell. He trailed every steer that went into the badlands, trying to prove that Dell was rustling just as his brothers had been. And every time he did that Dell hated him a little more. The drouth came, and of course Dell's cattle wandered down onto K Diamond for water. They had to, or die."

She sighed. "For a while your father simply drove them back. Then he began to build a drift fence."

I was incredulous. "On public domain?"

She nodded and said bitterly, "He calls it K Diamond, but it's public domain all the same. Over the past few years he's had members of his crew file on the water holes. He filed on the home place himself. But he couldn't fence the water holes against Dell's cattle without fencing out his own. So he built this drift fence, almost twenty miles long. He shut Purser and Dell off from water. Our cattle bunched on the fence and began to die. So Dell went out one night and cut the fence. I went with him. We cut the wire at every fifth post for twenty miles.

"Our cattle went through. But your father was furious about the fence. Dell forted up in the house for two days waiting for him. He expected the same sort of treatment your father gave his brothers. Instead, your father sent Roscoe Brady out with a warrant for Dell's arrest. Dell was going to shoot it out with Brady, but I persuaded him that would only make things worse for him. I convinced him that your father didn't have a case. K Diamond had fenced public domain when they had no right to. They couldn't convict Dell of fence cutting. Or at least that's what I thought. Now I'm not so sure."

I said vehemently, "They can't convict him!"

Rose smiled tiredly. "You're forgetting something. Your father owns the sheriff. Brady's bought and paid for. Your father was partly responsible for the appointment of Judge Franklin. If that isn't enough, he'll buy what other jurymen he has to buy, the same way he bought Brady. Ma and Longstreet and Purser and Delaney and most of the other cattlemen owe your father money."

I was full of youth's optimism and high ideals. I was outraged that Rose should be so desperate. I knew why she had come to me. She had loved me once and in her mind she still turned to me in spite of the shabby way I'd failed her. I forgot that taking my first case against K Diamond would be extremely foolish, and let myself get caught up with enthusiasm. I said confidently, "If he buys this jury he'll go to the pen for it."

There must have been a fire of conviction burning in my eyes. Rose looked at me for a long moment, and some of the hopelessness went out of her expression. She said, "Then you'll take the case?"

"Take it? You couldn't keep me away from it!"

Her eyes glistened. "I hoped you would. Thank you, Jeff." She got up and held out her hands. She squeezed one of mine hard between both of hers.

She said, "I'll talk Dell around to the idea of having a King for a lawyer. You wait until tomorrow and then come see him, will you, Jeff?"

I said I would, and Rose went out smiling hopefully.

I sat there frowning for a little while. Then I went to work on getting Dell out on bail, figuring Ma Peckham would post it. . . .

I found Judge Franklin in the hotel bar. He was a short,

portly man, who wore a Havana cigar in his mouth as habitually as most men wear a shirt. I couldn't remember ever having seen him without it. His clothes were tight-fitting and a little untidy. At his fat neck he wore a black string tie. His tiny eyes seemed lost in the folds of flesh around them.

He put out his hand and clasped mine heartily, "Jeff! By hell, boy, it's good to see you. Lawyer now, are you?"

I said I was, that I'd passed the bar and was going to practice in Arriola. I told him my first client was Dell Anson, and his face sagged with surprise. I said, "I want you to grant bail. Ma Peckham will post it. Dell's got work to do around home and can't waste his time lying around the jail. What the devil's he doing in jail anyway?"

"Your pa signed a criminal complaint."

I said, "You set the bail and I'll see that it's posted."

The judge studied me carefully. "Rob ain't goin' to like you takin' cases agin' him."

"Set the bail." He shrugged ponderously. "Twenty-five thousand."

"On a fence-cutting complaint? Are you crazy?" I was incredulous.

He coughed and wheezed, "More to it than that, boy. Dell Anson's threatened your pa half a dozen times—in front of witnesses."

I argued, but I knew I was beat. I figured this was only the first round. I should have known right then how the cards would fall, but idealism hadn't yet come up against the blank wall of reality.

I went out into the hot, dusty street. The sun beat down with a merciless intensity. I went over to my office and spent the rest of the day preparing my brief. . . .

The following morning I visited Dell in the jail.

He seemed unchanged since the last time I'd seen him, at Manuel's grave, but now there was no wildness in him, only a slow, smoldering anger. His eyes seemed to glow as he looked up at me. I said, "Hello, Dell."

He grunted. I was full of excitement over my first case and right then I didn't see why he couldn't share it. He looked as though he'd already been convicted. I said, "Dell, I'm not K Diamond. I'm your attorney, and I'm going to get you acquitted."

He looked at me pityingly, which only made my determination stronger. He said sourly, "You're dreamin'. Judge Franklin belongs to K Diamond just as much as that red stallion does. Time they get through pickin' a jury, the jurymen'll belong to K Diamond too."

I said, "That's where I want you to help me. I'll challenge every juryman you think might be beholden to K Diamond."

Dell laughed.

I said, "Besides, Pa can't fence the public domain. It's illegal. I'll file a cross complaint, charging him with trespassing."

I was so earnest that Dell softened a little. But he didn't change his belief that the trial would be a legal farce. He said, "You go on back to Denver and set up your practice. There's only one kind of law in Arriola County—Rob King's law. You were there the night he hanged my brothers. You heard the sheriff promise me Rob would be tried. But was he ever tried? No, you're damned right he wasn't."

I tried to be patient with Dell. "All right. So Pa's been the law in Arriola County up to now. That doesn't mean he'll always be. Arriola County is under the same laws as Chicago or New York. There's got to be a time when Rob King abides by them the same as anyone else. I want to make that time come a little sooner than it might otherwise come. But you've got to help me."

His long mouth twisted into a wry grin. He said, "You need more than my help, Jeff. But I'll help you as much as I can."

I'd wondered what Rose had seen in Dell, and why she'd married him. Right now I stopped wondering. Dell should have hated me bitterly for my part in the hanging of his brothers. He should have hated me if only because I was Rob King's son. He must have been a little jealous of Rose's regard for me. But he was big enough to put these things aside and see what I was trying to do. He knew it was hopeless, and tried to tell me it was. But I wasn't yet ready to believe it.

On a scorching day in mid-July, the case came up for trial.

Chapter Twelve

I'LL NEVER FORGET that day as long as I live—its oppressive heat, the dryness of it that made my skin burn, its bitter humiliation.

In the early morning, the town began to fill with folks from the far ends of Arriola County. Dust raised in a thick cloud from the street, and each patch of shade had its collection of idlers, waiting for court to convene at ten o'clock.

I visited Dell in his cell at nine-thirty and then went over to the courthouse. As I walked I could feel the amused stares of every group I passed, and once I heard the comment, "The whelp is goin' to take a lickin' today."

I was angered, and I was beginning to feel the frustration of opposing Rob King.

I'd challenged jurymen for the past three days. I'd challenged every person who could conceivably have owed anything to Rob King or K Diamond. But I knew I'd failed. For one thing, Judge Franklin had overridden a great many of my objections. For another, there simply wasn't a large enough panel of veniremen to pick twelve wholly impartial jurymen.

If the country had been afraid of K Diamond, things might have been different. But Pa couldn't possibly hurt any of his other neighbors by fencing, and even those who didn't owe K Diamond anything at the moment hoped for favors from Pa in the future.

I know Judge Franklin was right in what he told me that morning. "You should've started smaller, Jeff. You should've settled for drawin' up wills an' deeds for a while. Later, you'd of been ready fer a big case. You ain't right now, that's all."

He was saving his pride, his shame because he knew he'd let himself be bought—laying the blame for my failure on me, when in reality it lay upon his own dishonesty and that of the jurors.

I suppose I knew I was licked before I ever entered the courtroom that morning. I just wouldn't admit it.

Pa hadn't bothered to appear in town at all previous to the trial. He was not yet there when I arrived at court that morning. I knew how and when he would appear. He'd time his arrival so that he came in just after Judge Franklin had called the court to order. That way, he'd create a big stir, and would show his contempt for this small case that he knew was in the bag.

I wasn't wrong. Judge Franklin, with the ever-present cigar rolling back and forth from one side of his mouth to the other, banged his gavel, glared at the noisy crowd, spat at the spittoon beside him and said, "Court is now in session." He paused, and it was at that moment that Pa came in, looking faintly amused.

The courtroom buzzed, and heads craned to look at him. From him all eyes turned to me, and I fought the flush that rose to my face. Pa looked at me and winked solemnly.

When Pa was seated, Judge Franklin banged his gavel for order. "This case involves some fence-cuttin' by Dell Anson. Ain't no doubt but what Dell's guilty. Thing you got to decide is did he have a right to cut another man's fence so's his cattle could get to water. Bailiff, bring in the prisoner."

I thought angrily, "Hell, this man's no judge! He's a backwoods bumpkin. He's already prejudiced the jury."

The bailiff, in everyday life a swamper at one of the

saloons, brought Dell in and showed him where to sit. The trial, if it could be called that, proceeded.

Jennings Bruce, an immensely tall, stooped old man who somehow reminded me of Martin Longstreet, presented his case with surprising dignity under the circumstances. I got up and made my defense.

I was thoroughly scared inside, but I think I managed to conceal it.

I questioned Dell perfunctorily, and then I called Pa to the stand.

"Will you state your name?"

"Hell boy, you know my name. It's the same as yours." The courtroom roared with laughter and I turned red with anger. Pa's eyes looked at me with a veiled apology, as though he were saying, "I'm sorry, Jeff. But you shouldn't have taken the case."

I controlled myself and said, "This fence—was it on your land?"

"It ran along the edge of the badlands. Everything this side of the badlands is K Diamond."

"But you have no legal title, isn't that true?"

He grinned. "Let somebody try to take it and they'll damn soon find out whose land it is."

"In reality it's public domain. Isn't that true?"

"If you mean by that the public can use it, I reckon it ain't true. It's K Diamond, boy. It always will be."

I tried patiently to bring out that Pa owned only a few water holes scattered across K Diamond's endless miles of range. I brought it out, but both jury and courtroom disregarded the point. They clung to the old cattleman's belief that what he held was his. Public domain was a phrase to substantiate a distant government's claim on the land—nothing more. These people refused to recognize that claim, even those who held no land.

When I let Pa get down, I knew I was licked.

He tried to spare my feelings. During recess for dinner, he came to me and stuck out his hand. He said, "Why the hell didn't you let me know you were in town? I want you out at K Diamond. You belong there. It's yours as much as it is mine. Whichever way this damned case goes, I want you back home."

He spoke loud enough so that he was plainly heard by everyone within a ten-foot radius.

I went out to dinner with Rose. I think she knew my thoughts, for she was silent and subdued.

The afternoon was pure formality, as cut and dried as though the verdict were understood by everyone in the courtroom. The jury went out and the courtroom emptied. Rose went over to the jail to be with Dell.

Late that afternoon court convened and the jury foreman gave the verdict, "We reckon Dell Anson cut Rob's fence, all right. We figure he didn't have no right to cut it, either."

Dell got a year and a day. And I knew I was through as a lawyer in Arriola.

I'm not proud of myself for going back to K Diamond. But I did. Like a whipped pup, I tucked my tail between my legs and went home. Maybe I'd lost my young idealism, my faith in the law which had grown in me so steadily over the past several years. Maybe I just wasn't up to taking such a defeat so soon.

Judge Franklin had been right. I never should have taken the case.

I despaired of seeing law come to Arriola County, and for escape threw myself into ranch work as I never had before. I know I was sullen toward Pa, though I tried hard not to be. I know I thought of little else but my hatred of him. I dreamed of the day when I'd beat him, but they were empty dreams with no real hope of fulfillment.

The summer passed and roundup came, and after that Pa went to Chicago with the cattle, which filled three trains of more than thirty cars each.

All that fall I rode with a feeling of guilt over Rose and Dell Anson. Dell had been hauled off to the territorial prison shortly after the trial to serve out his sentence and Rose had gone back to his place in the badlands to try and hold things together until his return.

Not long afterward we had a three-day rain, which relieved my guilt to some extent, for I knew at least that their cattle were no longer suffering.

There came a time, however, while Pa was in Chicago, when I could no longer stand the realization that I'd failed Rose after promising so confidently to help her, and I had to know how she felt about me. I had to know whether she blamed me as bitterly as I blamed myself. And so, one morning in October, I rode over to see her.

I am aware now that deep in my subconscious mind I knew that my desire to see her stemmed more from my thinking of her as a woman than from my sense of guilt.

I couldn't admit it, even to myself, but I was in love with Rose, and always would be. I wanted her, and she belonged to a man who already had more than ample cause to hate K Diamond and everything connected with it.

Riding over to see her was foolish, and I knew it was. Half a dozen times since the trial, I had saddled and ridden toward the badlands, only to turn back. Today I didn't turn back. I rode into their yard just after nine o'clock.

This was the first time I'd been here since the awful night when Rolie and Clay had been hanged, and Manuel killed. The cabin seemed unchanged except for bright curtains at its windows and a general air of tidiness it had not had before. Down by the water hole the cottonwood stood, shedding its bright yellow leaves. In my mind, I could still see the two twisted bodies, their heads cocked as though listening for some slight sound, their unnaturally elongated bodies turning slowly.

It is hard to describe my feelings as I sat there. I finally admitted to myself that I wanted Dell's wife, and that my coming was the first step in my attempt to take her from him. The shame I had felt over failing Rose and Dell at the trial was doubled because of it.

I cleared my throat and called, "Hey! Anybody home?"

The door opened and Rose stood framed in it, her sombre face lighting instantly in a way that made my heart leap. Her eyes sparkled and a smile came to her lips. "Jeff! Oh, Jeff!" Almost immediately, however, the smile faded from her face. "You shouldn't have come."

"No. I know I shouldn't." Her thoughts and mine were the same at that instant. Dell was away in prison. If someone should see me here—if folks knew I'd come to see Rose . . .

I dismounted, and Rose shrank back a little into the doorway. I said, "I won't stay. But I had to see how you were getting along. I guess I had to know whether you hated me for failing you."

Her eyes brightened with unshed tears. Her voice was uncertain but strong. "I'm getting along fine, Jeff. Jim Purser helped me with roundup and shipped our cattle with his. And you know I could never hate you. What happened wasn't your fault. You did your best. No lawyer could have beat what you had to beat."

We stood ten feet apart, looking at each other. A flush stole slowly into Rose's face and she asked quickly, "What are you doing now, Jeff?"

"I'm not lawyering, if that's what you mean. Losing Dell's case finished me in Arriola. I'm back at K Diamond." I said it defiantly, not because I felt Rose would be critical, but because I was so ashamed of it.

I had to keep talking or I knew I'd close the distance between us. I said, "Rob's gone to Chicago with the cattle. Otherwise things are about the same. You had plenty of water since the rain?"

"Yes. We've had plenty." She chattered away almost feverishly, telling me of her single trip to Arriola a month or so ago, of the small things she had bought, of Dell's letters from the prison, bitter, angry letters that her own cheerful ones failed to change. She told me of his threat—to get Rob King as soon as he was released.

Yet all the time she talked, my mind was not on her words but on her mobile face with its wide cheekbones, on her bright, frightened eyes, on the golden hollow of her throat where an unnaturally fast pulse beat.

At last I said, "I won't come again, Rose."

Her eyes panicked. Then they went flat and dead, and her lips firmed out. She met my gaze steadily, hopelessly. "It would be best if you didn't. But thank you for coming today."

All I'd done for the past few years was to build walls between myself and this girl. I could have torn down the walls I'd built myself, but there was another wall now, one that could never be breached.

Mounting my horse was one of the hardest things I had ever done. I looked down at her from the saddle and my voice sounded strange, almost cold. "Good-by, Rose."

She looked lost, and helpless, and hurt. "Good-by Jeff."

I turned my horse and rode away. I looked back as I topped the first rise. She stood in the yard watching me. The breeze whipped her long skirt against her, outlining her straight, proud body. It whipped her midnight hair out behind her high-held head.

Movement caught my eye beyond the cabin and I saw Jim Purser riding in from the opposite direction.

My first impulse was to turn my back and set my spurs. I caught myself and raised my hand to Jim in a casual salute, which he returned, but not immediately.

I headed for K Diamond, determined that I'd never return here again, and hoping that Purser would have enough sense to keep his mouth shut about seeing me. . . .

Pa returned from Chicago that same day. An hour behind him came a caravan of wagons loaded with lumber, paint, furniture, draperies, everything imaginable that would brighten and make more livable the rambling adobe house at K Diamond.

The old house underwent a transformation, and a week after it was finished, Dolly came.

I'd known, of course, what the preparations meant, and had heard from Ches that Rob had met and married a woman in Chicago, and that she was coming to K Diamond in three weeks.

I expected another Annie, so I could not have been more surprised than when I walked over to the buggy in which Pa had driven Dolly from town.

She was a tiny woman, her head coming barely to Pa's solid shoulder. Pa reached up, and with his two big hands at her slender waist, swung her to the ground.

Her tiny feet seemed to take root instantly on K Diamond soil. She looked around at the sprawling, ugly adobe buildings, and out across the bare miles of K Diamond range, her face rapt. She said in her clear, cool, delighted voice, "Rob, you didn't tell me it was beautiful."

Pa said, "It ain't. It's K Diamond," as though that were more than being simply beautiful. "As far as you can see it's K Diamond." He spoke with the same sort of native pride with which a man says, "I am an American," or "I am an Englishman."

I stood there, awkwardly waiting for them to notice me. Dolly turned, raised her face to look at me and said, "Jeff? Is this Jeff?"

I nodded and was astonished when she rushed to me, threw her arms around my neck, and planted a soft kiss on my wind-roughened cheek.

She was small, so delicate you thought of her as being fragile. Her hair was a gleaming, lustrous copper, worn in a mass of ringlets behind her head. Her eyes were gray-green like the spring brightness of sagebrush leaves. A small bridge of freckles stretched across her nose.

I held her awkwardly for a moment while she hugged me, and from my father heard his great, booming laugh, the one I hadn't heard for many years.

Dolly stepped away, smiling happily, friendly as a puppy and as naively honest. I liked her at once. No one could help liking Dolly.

Chester Wolfe came from the bunkhouse and began to unload bags from the buggy, helped by one of the crew. He kept watching Dolly furtively, in an almost trancelike way.

Pa started toward the house, with Dolly walking beside him—or rather frolicking beside him, for that was the way she seemed to walk.

They disappeared into the house and Chester Wolfe went in behind them, his arms loaded with valises and bags. The cowboy who had been helping went out to harness the buckboard so he could go to Arriola after her trunk.

From the open door I heard Dolly's happy voice,

exclaiming in an excited, wholly childlike way. A few moments later I heard her squeal with joy as little Lee was brought out to her, and after that heard Lee's high, treble laughter.

Dolly alighted on K Diamond that morning like a bright bird, instantly charming every living thing she touched.

I remember being mildly amazed that Pa could have captured her. He was as big, rough and direct as the bare range of K Diamond, but I suppose enough of the gallant courtesies bred in him back home remained to charm this delicate creature into marriage after what must have been a headlong, whirlwind courtship.

I know now that I underestimated my father and his attraction for women just as I underestimated a great many of his other qualities. Over the years he had become but one thing in my mind, a harsh, cruel, unbending figure that ruled K Diamond as though it were some kind of crude frontier principality. I know now, too, that much of my hatred of father was based on jealousy because he had none of my doubts and fears and uncertainties, and because he was always able to beat me at everything I tried to do

I stood in the yard, feeling lonely and excluded and jealous because Dolly was giving Pa more attention than she was giving me. I remember telling myself that I was being childish, but unable to drown the resentment that surged up inside me.

After a while I went out to the corral, caught up a horse, and rode out.

Riding somewhat aimlessly, I headed southward toward Sand Creek. In my gloomy mood, it seemed to me that everything I had done or tried to do had ended in failure.

Rose was lost to me, and whether I wanted her so desperately only because she was, or whether I truly loved her, I couldn't tell. My career as a lawyer was smashed, at least until I showed courage enough to pick up the pieces and start over somewhere else. Father, of whom I now realized I was extremely jealous, was taken by Dolly, who would absorb his entire time and attention. She could not fail to, being what she was. Absorbed in my thoughts, I paid no particular attention to the way I rode. And so, it was a complete surprise to me when I rode over a low rise and saw the wagon before me.

It was a nester wagon, similar to the one I'd seen on the street of Arriola several months before. Its bed, with the canvas top, sat flat on the ground, the running gear having been removed to haul lumber from town.

Three men were unloading the lumber. And over a fire near the wagon, two women were preparing a meal.

They saw me at almost the same instant I saw them. At once, two of the men disappeared behind the wagon. The other took a few steps toward me and stood facing me, legs spread, defiance written in every line of him. The women continued with their cooking, casting furtive, frightened glances at me. They knew they were on K Diamond range and they knew Rob King's reputation.

Keeping my hands plainly in sight before me, I approached the man. He was older than my father by at least five years. He wore a beard in which there was a liberal sprinkling of gray, and it covered most of his face, so that only his eyes and forehead were visible to betray his expression.

The eyes were black as bits of coal, rather close-set, and he had a huge, powerful body that was clad in ragged bib overalls. He wore an open sheepskin coat, and no gun.

Riding in, I stole several looks at the women. One of them was middle-aged, thin and bony and harsh of face. The other was a girl, pretty in a meek, frightened way. I half expected her to run as I drew closer.

The man said, "Howdy," his voice tentative and unfriendly. I nodded and asked, "Fixin' to settle here?"

"Yep. Filed on it two days ago in Arriola. Corners there, an' there, an' there, an' there." He pointed with a stubby, hairy finger to the four winds.

"Know where you are?"

He scowled at me. "I'm on land that belongs to the United States Gov'ment."

I smiled. I glanced at the wagon. The two men who had disappeared behind it now stood in sight, and each held a rifle. They were both younger copies of the older man.

I felt a certain pity for this family. I knew what my father would do as soon as he discovered their presence, but I did not try to tell them. Apparently they'd come into this with their eyes wide open, settling on K Diamond because it was the best land to be had, and fully realizing the risk they took.

The older man said, "I'm Dave Owens. Them are my

two boys, Frank an' Pete. Over there's Mrs. Owens, an' that there's my girl, Lillie."

I acknowledged the introductions. "I'm Jeff King." I leaned out of the saddle and extended my hand. Owens looked surprised and suspicious, as though this were some kind of trick, but in the end he shook my hand.

The woman at the fire spoke up in a high, ready voice, "Ask him, Pa."

He didn't look at her, but spoke to me with surly defiance. "I know my right. This here's land that's open for filin'. But she figures I ought to ask what K Diamond aims to do about it."

I said, "I don't speak for K Diamond. Only Pa does that. And I reckon you know what he's goin' to say."

He nodded ponderously, scowling. He said, "We'll fight. Me an' my boys is used to fightin'."

I muttered, "You'll have to," but I don't think he heard. The woman spoke again from the fire. "We'd be pleased to have you eat with us, Mr. King."

I wasn't particularly hungry, but I knew they'd take it amiss if I didn't accept. Folks like the Owenses seemed possessed of an almost fierce pride. I said, "Thanks. I am hungry," and got down off my horse.

We ate around the fire. I caught Lillie watching me several times fearfully, and smiled at her each time. She was the kind of girl that made a man want to protect her. She looked so helpless, and so eternally scared. I suppose living with the Owens men would frighten any girl, for they were a lusty, rawtempered bunch without a speck of gentleness in any of them. They seemed to have been cast

in the same mold, and even their gestures and manner-
isms were alike.

I finished eating the plate of beans and salt pork, drank
my coffee and got my horse.

Mrs. Owens came up to me timidly as I mounted, and
said, "You're goin' to tell your pa we're here, I reckon."

I shook my head. If there was to be more violence on
K Diamond I was damned if I was going to be responsible for it. "He'll find out soon enough."

Chapter Thirteen

PERHAPS DOLLY sensed the strain between Pa and myself.
She was a sensitive and perceptive woman, besides being
a beautiful and charming one. At any rate, she had not
been on K Diamond three days when one morning she
came to me excitedly, her eyes shining. "Jeff, we're
going to have a picnic. I want you to come."

I'd rather have begged off, but I didn't see how I
decently could. I had the feeling that I'd be invading Pa's
privacy if I went, that I'd be hurting Dolly's feelings if I
refused.

Her light hand was on my arm and she looked up at me
with all the expectancy of a child. I said, "Sure. I guess
so, if it's all right with Pa."

"It is. Come on. Franklin's frying chicken and it's
almost ready. If you'll hitch up the buckboard, we'll be
ready by the time you've finished."

I went out and hitched up a light, buckskin team. I
drove them over to the barn and backed them up the

buckboard, the same one I'd been driving the day I caught K Diamond's Apache. It had a new coat of paint and was the best handling rig we had on the place.

When I drove up to the door, Dolly was waiting with a covered picnic basket. She was as excited as a child, chattering incessantly as she piled coats and blankets into the back of the rig. "The chicken's still hot. I wrapped it in a dish towel so it'll stay that way. I've got a jug of coffee and a pot to heat it in."

I asked, "Where's Pa?"

"He's coming." She climbed up on the seat beside me and snuggled over close to me to make room on the seat for Pa, who was just coming out the door. Pa looked at me and grinned and then he climbed up too.

I was amazed at the difference in him. He seemed younger by ten years. He looked down at Dolly, still grinning, and said, "So K Diamond comes to a standstill while we go off picnicking."

Dolly laughed, "Bosh! It runs itself." She took her attention from him and turned it to me. "It's time we got acquainted, Jeff. Don't you have a girl we could pick up and take along?"

I stammered something. Pa, still grinning, said, "He had one. But she married Dell Anson."

Dolly as quick to sense something wrong. I scowled at Pa, wondering how much he knew. I had a perverse desire to needle him as he was needling me. I could have, too, by suggesting that we drive south toward Sand Creek and pick my girl up. Lillie wasn't my girl, but it tickled me to imagine what Pa's face would look like when he saw squatters on K Diamond range. Yet I knew that wouldn't be fair to anyone, least of all the Owens family, so I held my tongue.

Dolly said reproachfully, "Rob, stop teasing him. He's been away to school. I'll bet he's got just lots of girls up there in Denver. And he will have here, too, if you'll just give him time. Won't you, Jeff?"

I was beginning to wish I hadn't come. Pa was paying me back for my surliness over the past couple of months. Maybe he'd keep at it all day. And maybe I'd reach a point where I didn't want to take it any more, in spite of Dolly.

But I was mistaken. That was the last barb he threw at me.

We drove north all morning and at noon stopped in the shadow of El Espalto de Cerdo. There were a lot of nice places to picnic up that way, places where cottonwoods grew thick and threw dark, cool shadows on the grassy ground.

While Pa and Dolly unloaded the buckboard, I unharnessed the horses and picketed them out to graze. Dolly spread a blanket on the ground and unpacked the picnic basket. We built a fire and heated the coffee, and afterward sat around and ate until we were stuffed.

Dolly picked up the picnic things and returned them to the basket, and Pa took a blanket and went off a ways to stretch out under a tree. Before long, he was snoring lustily.

Dolly smiled at him fondly, but when she turned back to me her face was serious. "Why do you two fight each other, Jeff?"

I tried to evade. "We don't fight."

"No. Not with your fists. But you fight with your minds—with your ideas."

I said, "I can't defend my side of it without criticizing him. Let's talk about something else."

"No." She was firm. "Tell me what you want out of life, Jeff. Isn't K Diamond enough?"

I thought about that for a moment. K Diamond wasn't enough—at least K Diamond as I'd always known it. But it could be enough, if Pa didn't set it above the law.

I said slowly, "Maybe I can see ahead. Maybe I can see the time when the law will be stronger than K Diamond. If he realizes it when that time comes, everything will be all right. But I know him too well. I know how stubborn he can be. He'll never admit that the law is stronger. He'll fight it. And if I'm still here I'll be in the middle, either on the wrong side because I'm his son, or on the right side, and forced to fight my own father. I don't want to get in that position."

I knew Dolly would try to draw me out further if I stayed and talked to her. I knew she was only trying to patch up the rift between Pa and myself, but I felt dis-loyal for having talked as much as I had. So I got up and said, "I ate too much. I'm going to take a walk and work it off."

She knew why I was leaving but she didn't try to stop me. Her face was sombre, perhaps a little sad as I walked away.

I was gone for over an hour, just wandering around,

thinking. Coming back, I could hear father's shouting laughter, and Dolly's delighted squeals while I was still a quarter-mile from where they were.

I came into sight of our picnic ground, and halted suddenly. Pa and Dolly were skylarking around on the blanket like a couple of kids. As I watched, she quieted in his arms, and he kissed her, long and hard. I could hear her muffled protest, "Rob! Jeff will be coming back. Stop it. Please!"

Pa chuckled deep in his throat, but he didn't release her. There was fascination for me in watching, and a kind of guilty excitement. I forced myself to retreat a dozen steps, and then I began to whistle. When I came into sight of them again, Pa was walking toward the horses and Dolly was trying to repair the damage the tussle had done her hair.

I was silent all the way back to the house, but neither of them seemed to notice. Excitement brightened Dolly's eyes as she chattered away at Pa, and his face held an unusual amount of color.

"Damn them both!" I thought, and was instantly ashamed, because I knew I was only jealous.

At dusk we arrived home, and I put away the buckboard and unharnessed the team. I swore to myself that I'd never go with them again.

I didn't either. And to avoid Dolly's continuing invitations, I began to evade both her and Pa.

I'm sure that Pa heard of the Owenses within a week after they settled on K Diamond, but he gave no sign. He seemed to have forgotten that K Diamond existed, and if he thought of the ranch work at all it was only when Ches brought him some problem for decision.

He lived for Dolly, taking her for long horseback rides on warm days, staying in with her before the fire on rainy ones. He drove her to Arriola several times and each time they came back with the buggy loaded down with packages of all sizes and descriptions.

Nights, lying in my darkened room which was just down the hall from theirs, I would hear them murmuring, and laughing, and skylarking as they had that day on the picnic. Then a suspicious silence would fall over the house, and I would know they had gone to bed. I'd lie there and think of Rose, of that rainy day in the cedars. I'd go alternately hot and cold. I'd long desperately for her warmth here beside me. And I'd know a bleak despair because I could never have her.

I believe that for those few weeks, Pa completely forgot my mother, the circumstances of her death and the obsession that had ridden him these many years. His great, booming laugh filled the house. He got so he had a slap on the back and a friendly greeting for me each time he encountered me. He showed a surprising tenderness toward Dolly and a renewed interest in little Lee, now a rowdyish youngster of almost five who had a genius for perilous adventures such as walking unconcernedly through a corral full of biting, kicking, half-broken horses, or climbing to the roof of the house and falling off into a barrel of rainwater.

The reason I believe he knew about the Owenses was that Dolly did. She came to me one day during one of

Pa's rare absences and said excitedly, "Jeff, I want to see our neighbors. Rob won't take me, so I want you to."

I said, "Pa won't like it."

"Fiddlesticks. Are you going to take me, or do I have to go by myself?"

"I'll take you." I went out to the corral and hitched up the buggy. When I drove it up before the house she came out. I helped her in, and she was light and airy as a bird.

As I drove across the bare, open prairie, she chattered delightedly to me, about my career which would have to be resumed in some large city where I'd not be hampered by local prejudices, about little Lee, who must attend a good agricultural college somewhere when he was old enough.

Knowing of the strain between my father and myself, she tried very hard to make me see his good qualities and gentleness, which he had shown her, but which I knew he'd never shown to another living soul except perhaps my own mother.

She drew me out by her rapt listening to every word I had to say, and with some surprise I found myself telling her of our home in the south, and the circumstances of our leaving.

"What a terrible story! But it's wonderful, wonderful, what you two have been able to do here."

I didn't tell her how it had been done. I didn't mention that Pa's first two herds had been stolen, the first at the cost of a bullet wound in his shoulder, the second at the price of three men's lives.

Neither did I mention K Diamond's Apache scourge,

nor the Anson brothers. She'd find out about these things soon enough, and about Dell Anson.

After two or three hours of driving across the prairie, we came to the Owens place.

They had a cabin framework up, and were working on the doors and windows. I could have told them they were making a mistake by building out of lumber when they could have more easily built out of adobe the way everyone else in the country did. I didn't tell them because it was none of my business. I didn't figure they'd be here long enough for it to matter anyway.

Dolly jumped from the buggy as soon as I stopped, and advanced to Mrs. Owens with both hands outstretched. "I'm Dolly King. Jeff tells me you are our nearest neighbors and I came to make you welcome and to say hello."

Mrs. Owens' mouth sagged open. She looked as though she were trying to make up her mind whether this was some kind of cruel joke, or whether Dolly was, unbelievably, serious.

I wandered over to watch the building and stood in silence while the Owens men cast unfriendly, suspicious glances at me. Dolly moved out of earshot to the Owens wagon with Mrs. Owens and Lillie.

Since I made no headway with my conversational overtures I left the half-finished shack and wandered back to the buggy where I waited comfortably in the sun.

I rolled and smoked three cigarettes. As I was finishing the third, Lillie Owens came timidly toward me, carrying a cup and a steaming pot of coffee.

She reminded me of a rabbit, terrified and not knowing

which way to run. Yet there was a certain softness about her that was very appealing.

She murmured in an almost soundless voice, "Ma says you might like some coffee."

I got up, towering almost a foot above her. I took the cup and she poured it full. I said gravely, "Thank you," and sipped the coffee dutifully.

We stood together in awkward, painful silence. At last she asked, "You goin' to let us stay here?"

"I haven't anything to say about it, Lillie. I guess it'll be up to Pa. If I were you, though, I wouldn't count on it."

"It's free land, ain't it?"

"Legally, yes."

"Then why can't we stay?"

I grinned at her ruefully. "That's a good question, but a little hard to answer. I suppose because Pa is stronger than the law in Arriola County. Some day that's going to change, but it hasn't come yet."

"Pa and the boys aim to fight. You going to fight against us?"

"No." I shook my head. "I'll not fight against you. K Diamond has a crew of fifteen men. They won't need me."

Dolly came walking with Mrs. Owens, chattering vivaciously to the older woman, whose face had lost its harshness and suspicion. I remember thinking that Dolly could charm a stone lion if she put her mind to it.

Dolly gave me her hand and let me help her into the buggy. "I'll come again, Martha, if you'll let me. K Diamond is an empire of men, and it's so good to talk to a woman again."

"Yes. Do come. Come real often."

We drove away. Going back, Dolly chattered at me again, but this time she talked of the Owens family, and how wonderful it was going to be when there were more settlers, when there were roads and schools and windmills, and barbed wire fences. I shuddered inwardly, wondering what would happen if she talked this way to Pa.

Apparently she did not mention the Owens family to him at all. For there developed no change in their almost idyllic relationship. . . .

For more than a month, Dolly managed at least one visit a week to the Owens place. Their house was finished, and they began to plow. Dave Owens' contention was that plowed land retained moisture better than unplowed land, and that if he plowed now, in early winter, the ground would be wet enough in the spring to grow a crop of grain.

Pa studiously ignored the Owens family, although I was sure he was aware of them. Now I know that he was simply too happy with Dolly to risk anything that might caused dissension.

I also knew he could not ignore the problem forever, because Arriola was filling with settlers, and the camp among the cottonwoods down near the Arriola River was assuming the proportions of a town itself. Every train brought more, and daily they streamed into town in their battered canvas-topped wagons.

In reality it was only a small part of a mass migration. From Texas to Montana the nesters were flowing in, settling on land which had never grown anything but grass, plowing it, getting ready to sow their crops. Some were dying under the cowmen's guns, giving up under their threat. But some were winning, and clinging like leeches to the land the Government said was theirs for the taking. The cattlemen won and lost, in a seesaw battle that went on all during the fall and early winter.

And Pa and Dolly lived out their precarious time together, with Dolly becoming gradually more silent and strained over what I believe she knew must eventually happen. She seemed more demanding of him, more savagely affectionate than she had ever been before.

I shook my head, knowing Pa much better than Dolly did, knowing that before spring something terrible would happen to us all, something that would tear us apart and perhaps destroy us forever.

And as Dolly became more attached to Martha Owens, so did I become attached to Lillie.

Perhaps I did so because I knew I could never have Rose. Perhaps Lillie was simply consolation for my frustrated heart. But I didn't realize it at the time, and so we moved into the winter, playing our parts like puppets and with no more apparent control over our movements and desires than wooden figures at the end of a string.

Chapter Fourteen

IN MID-DECEMBER, returning from an aimless ride, I

hauled my horse in at the top of a low rise and sat looking down at the house. There were dust trails approaching K Diamond from all directions, visible for miles in the still, clear air.

My old foreboding stirred, for I knew what the dust trails meant. There could be but one explanation for the arrival of all our neighbors at once. They had come to make their inevitable demand, and knowing Pa, I was aware that he could not refuse. I saw him come out onto the great, long gallery and stand there greeting them one by one as they came into the yard.

My first impulse was to ride to the Owens place with a warning. But I knew, even as the impulse struck me, that the time was not yet. Instead, I headed down the rise toward the house. I rode to the corral and turned my horse in. I took a great deal more time than was necessary putting away my saddle, bridle and blanket.

Finished, and frowning, I walked reluctantly across the yard. I saw Delaney's yellow-wheeled buckboard, and guessed that Frank had brought his wife to visit with Dolly. I saw Purser's big black saddle stallion, and old Martin Longstreet's blooded sorrel mare. There was a buggy too, its paint cracked and peeling, that I guessed belonged to Rose's mother, Mrs. Peckham.

Stepping onto the long gallery, I took off my hat and automatically batted the dust from my clothes. I felt almost physically cold, although the day was unseasonably warm. I suppose I suspected, even then, that today would see an open break between my father and Dolly, and probably between Pa and myself as well.

I went in, and greeted everyone almost absently, my eyes on my father. He seemed uneasy, and angered because he was. I believe he knew what was shaping up, and what its consequences would be.

Dolly's face held a flush of excitement, and her eyes were shining with delight. She was reveling in the pleasure of so much company all at once and I remember thinking, "Pa should have had folks in before. He's been keeping her too much to himself."

Dolly really blossomed in a crowd of people. She chattered incessantly. I could see from our neighbors' expressions that every one of them had fallen in love with her instantly; and yet there seemed to be a certain reserve in them all.

Why Dolly didn't feel this, I can't imagine, as sensitive as she was to the moods of people around her. Possibly she thought they were simply uneasy at getting acquainted with K Diamond's mistress for the first time.

At last she said, "I'll fix some coffee," and went into the kitchen. Pa watched her go. I could not misinterpret the look his eyes held—loneliness, desperation, a kind of hunger. The look vanished as Bess Delaney, a plump, motherly woman, got up from the sofa and went across to Pa. She took his hand in her own two hands and said, "She's lovely, Rob. You're a lucky man. But don't be so darned stingy with her. Let us see her once in a while."

Pa's face twisted into what he meant to be a grin. He said, almost absently, "I will, Bess. I will."

Bess's smile mocked him good-humoredly; then she murmured, "I'll go help her in the kitchen. Get on with your man-talk."

She left, rustling pleasantly in her satin gown, and Pa sank down onto a leather-covered platform rocker. He stared across at me, and I met his glance coldly. In my mind I was seeing the Owens shack reduced to charred embers, seeing the bodies of the Owens men strewn awkwardly around in the yard.

For the first time in my memory, Pa's glance wavered before my own. He was a changed man from the implacable, selfconfident man I remembered. Dolly had done that. He was afraid—afraid of losing her. For the first time his guns and his ruthlessness and the blue flame in his eyes were not enough to hold what was his.

Longstreet was talking with his slow and measured amiability. "It's sure been dry, ain't it Rob? Too damned dry. Time we got a storm."

Delaney broke in nervously, "We'll get it, Mart, don't worry about that. Bess claims she can tell when a storm's brewin' by watchin' the chimney smoke. If it goes down from the chimney an' rolls along the ground, then a storm's comin', accordin' to her. Anyhow, that's what it was doin' this mornin'.""

Pa nodded, but I could tell his mind wasn't on the conversation. He kept glancing at the kitchen door. His body seemed tense with waiting, tense with foreboding and uncertainty.

Longstreet said finally, "Well, I reckon you know why we came, Rob."

Pa started, and his attention instantly focused on Longstreet. He said with surprising quietness, "The

Owens bunch?"

"That's right." Longstreet got to his feet. His face, incredibly ugly, possessed a peculiar attractiveness because it was so ugly. His eyes were fierce as an eagle's as he looked at Pa. "The time's run out, Rob. I never thought anyone would have to tell you to run someone off K Diamond, but it looks like that's what we've got to do."

A wild kind of anger flared in Pa's eyes. I felt like laughing, and was instantly ashamed. But Pa controlled himself with obvious difficulty and remained silent, waiting.

Longstreet went on, his voice deeply concerned, "I was in town the other day. The cottonwood grove down below town looks like an army camp, what with tents and wagons and fire goin' all the time. There must be two hundred people there."

Delaney broke in, "They're restless, Rob. So far just knowing your reputation has been enough to keep them off. But Owens hasn't been touched, and the rest of them are getting brave. You hold off another two weeks and they'll swarm over the range like locusts. And it ain't only K Diamond they'll settle on; they'll settle on us too."

Pa shot a glance at me, then he looked at the kitchen door. Pressure was closing in on him from all sides. He knew I'd been seeing Lillie Owens. He knew that Dolly had been calling regularly on Mrs. Owens, and that Dolly liked her. But he also knew that these men, his friends and neighbors, were counting on him. He said, a shade defensively, "I was figurin' on runnin' them off."

"When? We can't wait any longer, Rob. Owens has been talking to that bunch in town—about God intending this land to be used for crops. Every time he talks to them they're a little closer to moving out on the range. They've hung back so far on account of the threats we've all been making, but they won't hang back forever. If you don't do somethin' about Dave Owens and them two over-grown sons of his, we'll all be finished."

Pa said heavily, "You know Dave Owens. You know damned well you're telling me to kill him."

So Pa did know Dave Owens—even to his character. I'd underestimated him.

Longstreet shrugged. His eyes were like ice. He growled, "Marriage must've made you soft, Rob. You didn't need anybody to tell you what to do about the Anson boys, nor about them 'Paches what run off your horses that time."

Pa's fists balled, but I felt no sympathy for him. Longstreet smiled grimly, adding, "Hell, what happens is up to Dave Owens, ain't it? He doesn't have to fight."

"But he will. You know he will."

"So he'll fight. We've talked it out among ourselves, Rob. You move him or we'll do it for you."

Pa might have argued further, but Dolly came in from the kitchen carrying a tray upon which were cups and a pot of coffee. She busied herself distributing the cups and filling them. Bess Delaney brought in a cake and fol-lowed her, passing it around.

I noticed that Dolly's smooth face was strained, that her

eyes were scared and not at all friendly as she looked at Longstreet. Dolly must have overheard Longstreet's demands.

I watched Pa, seeing the way his anger was mounting. Pressure had made him furious, but he held his peace, listening to the small talk that was now passing back and forth in the group. Time passed, nearly half an hour of it, and at last Bess Delaney said, "Frank, it's time we were going."

The men of the group, and Mrs. Peckham who had talked but little, got up with obvious relief and went to the door. I heard Bess Delaney say to Dolly, "Now you make that husband of yours bring you over for a visit. He can't have you to himself forever."

The group surged out onto the gallery. Perhaps they would have left with no more talk of the Owens family. But Pa caught them before they could disperse. "How about the rest of you? You all feel the same way Longstreet does about this?" he asked.

Delaney nodded. He said, "It ain't exactly a question of how we feel, Rob. It's a question of what we got to do. Rightly, it's your problem because the Owens outfit is squatted on your range. But it's our problem too. It's every cowman's problem. We've fought too long and too hard for our land to give it up now. Maybe the damned plowmen won't stay. Probably they'll quit the first time a dry year comes along an' go looking for something easier. But they'll tear up the land. They'll string their fences an' build their shacks an' plow up the grass. They'll live off our beef whilst they're here. Rob, I for one ain't goin' to stand for it. Not even if I have to move Dave Owens myself."

Mrs. Peckham, sixty if she was a day but strong and leathery as a man, said in her dry voice, "It's a hard thing to do, Rob, but it's got to be done. You know it as well as we do."

She looked strange to me in her cotton dress. I'd seldom seen her in a dress. Mostly she wore men's clothes, and on roundup there were times when I forgot she was a woman, so completely did she forget it herself. I wondered if she had been as beautiful as Rose when she was young.

Pa looked at Purser, who had been watching me strangely as Mrs. Peckham spoke. I knew Purser was thinking of the time he'd caught me leaving Rose's place. Purser and Pa were on bad terms since Pa's fencing off the badlands. Now Purser said sullenly, "I feel the same way they do."

The easy way out for Pa would have been to refuse, to let his neighbors move the Owens outfit themselves, and yet even this would not have relieved him for responsibility in Dolly's eyes, nor in mine.

He squared his tremendous shoulders and I knew what he was going to say. My stomach felt empty, cold. Whether Dolly and I liked it or not, he'd move the Owens outfit. If they fought him, as they surely would, then responsibility for whatever happened would, according to Pa's thinking, be squarely upon their own shoulders.

He said sourly, "All right. I'll take the crew over there in the morning. Owens will be gone by tomorrow night."

Dolly was silent as she stood at his side on the gallery and watched our guests depart. Longstreet rode out first, and Delaney followed. Suddenly then they were all gone and the yard was quiet save for a cackling chicken.

Pa slipped an arm about Dolly's slim waist, but she seemed stiff and unyielding. He said, "I haven't been very fair to you. You've missed seeing people."

"Not that kind of people." Her voice was cold and strained. Pa tried to draw her to him, but she pulled away. He asked stiffly, "What's the matter with them? They're good people, and they're my friends."

Dolly turned to him then, with defiant anger. Her eyes blazed and her cheeks were flushed. "Good people! They want you to murder the Owens family. Is that good?"

"Nobody said anything about murder. But Owens is camped on my grass. If he's allowed to keep it there will be half a hundred families on the land inside of two months. Come spring, there'll be five hundred more. Right now, Dolly, there are squatter families in every town within a hundred miles of here and they're waiting for just one thing—to see if Owens can stick. They've about decided he can, too."

Again I was aware that I'd underestimated Pa. He knew everything that was going on, in spite of his apparent pre-occupation with his new bride.

Dolly looked at him with quiet incredulity. "Well, I never! Do you mean to stand there and tell me you're actually going to do it? That you're going to try and drive these people away?"

"I'm not going to try. I'm going to do it." He shook his

head, helplessly. "Dolly, this is man's business. Stay out of it, like Bess Delaney does."

"I will not! And you ought to be ashamed of yourself! Suppose someone came here and told you to move out? Would you do it?"

Pa was pale. "Dolly," he said, "that's different."

"What's so different about it? This is your home and that shack is the Owens family's home. They'll fight for it just as hard as you'd fight for K Diamond."

"I'm hoping they won't fight."

"Oh Rob, how wrong can you be? You know what kind of man Dave Owen is. His sons are exactly like him. They'll fight as long as there's life in their bodies."

Pa's voice was stiff. "Then they'll fight. It can't be helped. But I'll run them off whether they fight or not."

"You wouldn't!" Dolly stared at him. "Rob, I thought I knew you, but I guess I was wrong. Surely you realize what will happen. They'll be killed!"

Pa said coldly, "This isn't Chicago. It's time you learned it."

"No. I see that it isn't." Dolly was very white now. Her lips were trembling. But her glance was steady enough, as though she had made up her mind definitely about something. "Rob, I'm warning you, don't do it. Because if you do, I'm going to leave you. I'm going back to Chicago."

She could have said nothing that would have had a worse effect on Pa. His voice was suddenly very hard. "That," he said, "is something you'll have to decide for yourself."

Leaving her standing there, he strode furiously across the yard toward the corral. He didn't look back. Angrily he saddled a horse, mounted, and raked furiously with his spurs.

The animal thundered out of the yard. Dolly looked at me. Her eyes were filled with hurt and bewilderment. She asked piteously, "Jeff, what have I done?"

I hated Pa in that moment more than I ever had before. I didn't say anything.

Tears brightened Dolly's eyes, and suddenly she turned and fled into the house.

I swore savagely to myself. Pa had at last met something he couldn't beat. By this time tomorrow, he would finally have lost something that was his, either K Diamond, or Dolly, and maybe both.

Chapter Fifteen

AT SUNDOWN, Chester Wolfe rode in from Arriola with two of the hands. He'd been there on some business of K Diamond's, I supposed, but when he'd put his horse away, he came directly to me instead of going in to report to Pa. His narrow face was worried, his gray eyes concerned.

Ches wasn't a big man, but aside from Pa, he was the hardest rider, the best roper, the deadliest shot on K Diamond. If anyone could have filled Manuel's shoes, it was Ches.

He said, "Jeff, I heard somethin' in town today. Dell Anson broke out of the pen."

I guess I didn't show enough concern to suit Ches, for he said then, "He's threatened to kill Rob. He's threatened to kill you, too."

"Me? Why me? Does he think I didn't do all I could at the trial?"

I still wasn't properly concerned about Dell's escape. It didn't seem possible that he could seriously consider trying to kill Pa, or me.

Ches coughed and looked embarrassed. "There's another story all over Arriola. It's that you've been hangin' around Dell's wife."

"That's a damned lie!" He had my attention now—all of it.

I must have looked ready to hit Ches, for he took an involuntary backward step. "Jeff, take it easy! I didn't start the damned story. I'm just telling you what I heard."

"It's still a dirty lie."

"You ever go over there to see Rose?"

I felt a sudden raw, wild anger. "You calling me a liar, Ches?" He looked at me closely. I calmed down and said, "I went over there once. Once is all."

"Somebody must have seen you."

"Purser rode in as I was riding out. I never got closer to Rose than ten feet, Ches, I swear it. I didn't even go in the house."

"That wouldn't matter to Purser. He hates Rob damn near as much as Dell does. Rob fenced him off from water too, you know. Purser lost about forty head of cattle. This is his way of getting back at K Diamond. He hasn't got the guts to do it the way Dell will, so he does it with talk." He hesitated. Then he said quietly, "Watch yourself," and turned to go toward the house.

I went over and climbed up on the corral fence. I made a smoke and lighted it. I wished I could straighten out my thoughts and feelings. Everything that had seemed so solid was going to pieces—Pa's and Dolly's marriage. K Diamond.

My head began to ache under the pressure of my thoughts. Pa was going to move the Owens family, and I couldn't stand by and let him. I didn't know whether I loved Lillie or not; it didn't really matter, I decided. I was still bound to try to keep Pa from killing any of her family.

And what about Dell? Suppose I did meet him somewhere? Could I draw a gun against Rose's husband, when I knew I'd done none of the things he thought I'd done? I tried to be honest with myself. Maybe I hadn't done anything, but I'd wanted to. Wasn't that just as bad?

I remember wishing desperately that day that I could be as confidently sure of myself as Pa had always been. Why couldn't I choose a course the way he did and follow it through to the bitter end? Why must I be forever torn between him, whom I both loved and hated, and a course I believed to be right but which threw me into open conflict with him?

I didn't know the answers, but I decided I'd just have to go along, doing what I believed right at the moment. Perhaps I'd make mistakes, and maybe in the end I'd know I'd been wrong. But at least I'd have no cause for shame, or regret.

Dolly didn't eat with us that night. Pa was silent and filled with surly anger. He scarcely spoke to me, except to ask once, "I suppose you feel the same way Dolly does about that damned bunch of rawhiders?"

I nodded, not trusting myself to speak.

"And what're you going to do about it?" he asked contemptuously.

I looked up at him, the things I felt plain in my eyes, and saw his anger leap. He half rose out of his chair and reached for me. But suddenly the strength seemed to drain out of him.

I thought, "I'll show you, damn you. I'll show you." This was the thought he had seen in my eyes, this and the defiance that went with it.

He got up and stamped out of the house. I knew I shouldn't have looked at him with hate showing in my eyes; if I couldn't respect him it was time I got out—clear away from both Pa and K Diamond.

But not yet—I couldn't run before Dell Anson's threat any more than I could run out on Lillie Owens. . . .

A wind came up during the night and howled around the house, pelting its windows with sand—a hot wind for December. I remembered Bess Delaney's prediction that a storm was coming, and finally dropped off to sleep, with the formless thought stirring in my mind that no storm could be as bad as the storm brewing right here inside this house.

Morning was still hot, but the wind had died during the

night. Over K Diamond hung an almost oppressive still-
ness. By the time I got up and arrived at the breakfast
table, Pa had gone outside. I could hear his voice in the
yard, bawling orders as he readied the crew for the trip to
the Owens place.

Dolly came in and sat down across from me. She
glanced at me with dull, hopeless eyes. Her voice was
almost a whisper. "I hope you slept better than I did, Jeff.
All night I lay awake, trying to decide."

I had always thought Dolly beautiful. But this morning
she seemed more beautiful than ever in a way that made
my throat feel tight. Her tiny body was dressed in a gray
woolen traveling suit. Her hair, bright copper and glossy
as silk, looked as though she had spent hours on it, but I
knew she had not. Her face was drawn and pale. She
murmured, speaking her thoughts aloud, "I can still stay
if I want to. It's not too late!" She looked at me plead-
ingly, "Tell me what to do, Jeff."

I smiled at her wryly. "How can I tell you what to do
when I don't know what to do myself?"

She reached over and patted my hand. "Poor Jeff. It's
been your problem much longer than it's been mine,
hasn't it? I heard about your Indian—and the Anson
boys."

Her sympathy made me feel foolish. We finished eating
and I went to my room after a coat. Almost without
thinking, I checked the loads in the old Dance Brothers
and Park revolver, then belted it around me. I slipped into
my coat, still hesitating over the course I would take, but
knowing anyhow I'd have to go along with Pa and the

crew to the Owens place.

I walked over to the window and stared into the yard. The rising sun was half obscured by a yellowish-purple haze that hung low on the distant horizon, reminding me again of Bess Delaney's storm prediction. A rider thundered in from the rolling, limitless expanse of K Diamond grass, driving before him a herd of galloping horses. Their manes and tails streamed out in the wind of their own making. They cavorted and bucked, kicked and squealed, but they came in and went without deviation into the old, crumbling adobe corral.

Before the bunkhouse, men rose to their feet from waiting, hunkered positions, hitched self-consciously at their shell-laden gunbelts and shook out the loops of their ropes. Then they moved toward the corral to rope out their mounts. I knew that I'd have to hurry.

I saw Pa come from the house and stride across the yard, a big man well over six feet tall, filling his plaid wool shirt until the seams stretched. His great tawny mustache stirred in a sudden gust of wind. He was tall and arrogant, as male as a scarred old range bull. His hair was like a lion's mane, uncut since his last trip to town, curly and glistening from its morning dousing with cold water from the pump.

Low against his lean right thigh rode his gun, supported by a shell-studded belt. His roaring voice shouted an unnecessary order, "Get your horses! Saddle up! Let's go!"

Hands on hips, strong legs spraddled, he stood and watched the hurried preparations. Doubt stirred in me, and an empty feeling came to my stomach. How could I face him when the time came? How could I stop him?

With a bullet, my thoughts answered. Only with a bullet.

I turned from the window and headed down the hall toward the big living room. Dolly came out of Pa's and her room ahead of me carrying a light valise. She was ten feet ahead of me. As she came into the living room, Chester Wolfe rose from the horsehair sofa and came toward her, thin-faced, whip-lean, his eyes holding an expression that halted me in my tracks. Was Ches in love with my father's wife?

I made no attempt to conceal myself, and he could have seen me if he'd looked. But he had eyes only for Dolly. He said slowly, "Let me get your things for you, Mrs. King."

I stepped back into my doorway as Ches came along the hall to get Dolly's other bags from her room. If he saw me, he gave no indication of it. I watched his face, shocked and unbelieving.

And suddenly I knew how wrong I was. Ches wasn't in love with her the way Pa was. Ches worshipped her, admired her, and he was furious because she was being hurt and because he was helpless to prevent it.

He got her bags and carried them into the living room, and then to the gallery outside. I heard his voice speaking to Dolly on the gallery, "I harnessed the buckboard for you. Rob says you can leave it in town at the livery barn. He'll have someone pick it up."

"Thank you Ches." There was a tremor in Dolly's

voice, as though she were struggling against tears.

Ches's voice sounded almost harsh. "You're a great lady, Mrs. King, the finest lady I've ever known. You an' Rob—well, hell. It ain't right this happenin' to you."

A dry sob caught in Dolly's throat, but she didn't reply.

I crossed the living room and went out onto the gallery. Ches's face was white with strain. I ran across the yard and got my saddle from the barn. I roped myself a mount quickly out of the remaining horses in the corral. I saddled, mounted, and rode back across the yard to the house.

The buckboard waited, hitched to our gentlest team of blacks. The crew was mounted, waiting. Pa turned from them and strode toward us.

His face was as cold as a winter wind, his eyes as bleak as a gray winter sky. He stopped and stared down at Dolly, without any change of expression.

He said coldly, "So you're going?"

"Yes, Rob."

"And you're not coming back?"

"No, Rob. You won't let me." She was white-faced, trembling, but her voice was firm.

Pa put his harsh glance on Chester Wolfe, standing just behind Dolly. I could tell from Pa's expression that he wanted to hurt something. Ches was handy. Pa asked, "Is he going with you?"

Dolly flushed painfully. "Rob! That's unfair!"

"Is it? Look at him. He looks at you like a dying calf."

Ches stepped forward, his fists clenched at his sides. His voice was tight, even, deadly, and it had its overtone of contempt. "How blind and stupid can a damn man get?"

Pa stared back at him, trying to beat him down with the impact of his eyes. At last he said with biting sarcasm, "Are you foreman of K Diamond, Mr. Wolfe? If you are, I'd suggest that you get your horse saddled and be ready to ride."

For a moment I thought Ches was going to throw his job in Pa's face. But the habit of loyalty was too strong. His glance shuttled angrily between Pa and Dolly and then he strode out stiffly across the yard.

Dolly broke the painful tension. "I thought you might give me a man to drive the buckboard, Rob."

He was like a small boy, defensive, knowing he was wrong but unwilling to admit his fault. "I need my men. I need them all."

"Yes. I suppose you do." There was no irony in her voice. But I couldn't help thinking, "He needs his men—all of them—to murder a man and two grown boys."

For the briefest instant there was regret, or pain, in Pa's face. The breeze, growing stronger, stirred his hair and disturbed his thoughts, whatever they had been. He growled, "I forgot my hat. Wait until I get it and I'll put your things in the buckboard for you."

He crossed the gallery and went hurrying into the house. In an instant he was back, hat crammed on his head. But I was already lifting Dolly's bags into the back of the buckboard. With Pa looking on, glowering, I helped her up onto the buckboard seat.

I was aware of the crew watching this from across the yard. Dolly took up the reins. Pa said quickly, almost desperately, "Your coat," and ran back into the house. He returned, carrying her wolfskin coat and handed it up to her. Dolly said, "Good-by, Rob."

He muttered gruffly, "Write me when you're settled. Send what papers need to be signed to me. I'll sign them."

I had the strange feeling that all this had happened before. And I remembered Annie's words to me so many years before, "When you come back again, I'll be gone." Annie had divorced Pa, and now Dolly was going to.

She said, "Yes. I know you will. Thank you, Rob."

They were like strangers. I saw the temper rise suddenly into Pa's eyes, a blue flame, and for the first time this morning he seemed to forget we had an audience. He said in a tight, angry voice, "We're being damned civilized about this, aren't we?"

She did not reply, but her body stiffened.

Pa glared at me, and then a pleading note crept into his voice, "Dolly, you're wrong about this. It isn't just the Owens tribe, can't you see that? It's not their lousy squatter's claim I'm worrying about today—it's K Diamond. You saw yourself how many squatters there were in Arriola last time we were in. It's just like that in every town within a hundred miles of here, and they're all waiting to see if Dave Owens can make it stick. Owens has become a symbol of resistance to them. If somebody doesn't do something about it, I'll have squatters camped on every square mile of K Diamond range. Dolly, try to see it my way."

It was the first time I'd ever heard him plead and I felt

sorry for him in spite of myself. But Dolly's small hands only closed tight on the edge of the seat until they turned white with the pressure. I knew she was very close to flinging herself into Pa's arms. She spoke in a still, small voice. "Rob, we went over it all last night. Those are people you're going to be killing today—not coyotes, or wolves, or lions."

Angry again, Pa growled, "You make it sound like they won't be given a choice. They don't have to fight."

Dolly sighed, releasing her grip on the edge of the seat. She murmured resignedly, "Rob, it's no use. Can't you see it's no use? You won't give an inch, and I can't. I can't."

Without speaking, he turned away from her. He strode across the yard and snatched the reins of his big roan horse from one of the crew. He mounted, and did not look back at Dolly or me.

His great cartwheel spurs drove deep into his horse's sides and the startled, frightened animal reared and pawed the air. Pa's fist clubbed down between the horse's ears with brutal violence. The roan dropped his forefeet to the ground, made a couple of crowhops, and began to run.

I said, "Good-by, Dolly."

There were tears streaming down her cheeks. She leaned toward me and threw her arms around my neck. "Good-by, Jeff."

I pulled away, my throat tight, the wetness of her tears cool against my cheek. I walked over to my horse and mounted. Looking down, I said, "I'll stop him if I can."

Dolly picked up the reins and slapped the backs of the horses with them. "I know you will, Jeff." And she drove away along the two-track road that led to Arriola. I spurred my horse southward in the wake of Pa and the galloping K Diamond crew.

Chapter Sixteen

AS I RODE OUT, I could see the crew ahead of me, pounding hard to keep up with Pa. Dust rose behind them in a cloud that the rising north wind pushed along behind like a pillar.

Glancing back, I saw Dolly driving away from K Diamond's sprawling adobe buildings, a lonely, diminutive figure, her back straight and her eyes ahead. As I watched, she stopped the buckboard and put on her wolf-skin coat. I realized how cold the wind had become. It must have chilled twenty-five degrees in the last few minutes.

The feeling of impending disaster was strong in me, the foreboding that had been troubling me the last couple of days. Everything took on a nightmarish quality in my mind, as though all this were not really happening at all. Pa and I had gone through plenty of things since that night back home when Mother had been killed. Most of them had bothered me, but nothing had ever bothered me in prospect so much as this trouble with the Owens family.

Nothing could stop Pa. K Diamond was his religion, holding it together his creed. He'd put aside his love for

Dolly in order to evict the Owens family. How could I expect to stop him? Could I draw and fire a gun against my own father? I doubted it. But I did know one thing— he would be stopped before he could injure a single member of Lillie Owens' family.

My thoughts drifted away from my father and centered themselves on Lillie. I tried to visualize her in my mind, but it was not she who appeared, but Rose's full-lipped mouth, her lovely eyes, her cascade of midnight hair. I shook myself savagely and made my mind go blank.

It took me almost half an hour to catch up with Pa and the crew. He rode at the head with Ches beside him. I noticed, as I rode up, that Ches was watching Pa with a look of utter incredulity. It was quite beyond Ches's understanding, I knew, that Pa would throw away such a precious thing as Dolly's love.

In the faces of the others was mostly uneasiness, caused in part by what they knew to be ahead, in part by the quarrel and separation of Dolly and Pa. In their minds they called him a fool. Most of them, I knew, were in love with Dolly, giving her the worshipping, sexless love of men whose contacts with good women have been limited largely to their mothers and sisters.

A loyal crew, they'd do as Pa told them to do. They would do it as bravely and efficiently as they could because of their loyalty to Pa and K Diamond. Where would they stand in a quarrel between Pa and myself? Neutral, I hoped.

Pa seemed immersed in his own bitter thoughts. As I rode up, however, he apparently realized that he was pushing his horse cruelly and unnecessarily. He reined in to a jogging trot. He also seemed to realize how cold it was getting. He wore no coat. In the turmoil of leaving, he had forgotten it.

He looked up at the sky, as though surprised, and I looked up too. The sun was a luminous ball, half hidden by the oddly colored mists that lay across the skies. It was ringed with vapor, a phenomenon I had never seen before. I'd seen a ring around the moon often, but never around the sun. All of us, including Pa, knew a storm was brewing.

In the southern part of Colorado Territory we had snows in winter, and occasionally a howling blizzard, but no storms in my memory had ever lasted more than a couple of days, or had been severe enough to cause hardship. Perhaps that's why none of us paid any particular attention to the signs forecasting this one.

Ches, who had fallen behind a little, now urged his horse abreast of Pa's. His voice was expressionless, his eyes flat and cold. "You forgot your coat. You'll miss it before the day's over."

Pa didn't answer. Wolfe looked at the sky again and said, "You should have given Mrs. King a man to drive for her. It's fifty miles to town. It'll be snowing like hell before she gets there."

Pa scowled. "You'd like to have gone, wouldn't you?" His voice was loaded with biting sarcasm. "Maybe you'd have just gone on with her. Maybe you wouldn't have come back."

Ches flushed darkly with anger. His mouth opened for

a savage retort, then closed like a trap. His hand clenched hard and a muscle along his jaw played briefly. But when he spoke it was calmly enough. "Don't blame your own failure on me. I admire your wife. I like her. But that's all. She's your wife. Even if I wanted to, which I don't, I'd never forget that—nor would she."

Pa reined over close of Ches. Their glances locked and held. Pa's face slowly lost its color. I didn't know whether he was going to hit Ches or draw his gun. He did neither.

Ches said slowly, evenly, "I wonder if you know just how much you've given up."

Pa's eyes fell away. He scowled, but I knew he was ashamed of needling Ches. Ches had taken Manuel's place in more ways than one, and today Ches was Pa's conscience. Pa hated him for it.

The inevitable had happened, as I'd known it must. Pa's creed of holding to what was his had at last come into conflict within itself. It had split, forcing him to a choice—the loss of either Dolly or K Diamond. I knew how hard the choice had been. His life and mind had been spent in building K Diamond. Now a rag-tag family of nesters threatened to tear it from us.

This was only one small fight between Pa and the Owens family, but the thing was larger than that. All over the great plains, ranchmen were fighting the same battle which Pa would be fighting today. They were fighting the tide of settlement, the relentless, remorseless encroachment of squatters who would like to see the range country churned by the plow.

This was what Pa had tried to tell Dolly. But Dolly, with her tender heart, had been able to see only the Owenses, struggling to build a home on land that the Government said they could have. She had been able to see only that the settlers would bring law with them, law for the masses, not law bought by lead from a six-shooter or paid for in cattlemen's gold.

A flake of snow stung my cheek. I brushed it away with my hand. Then another struck, and another. Suddenly the air around us was filled with snow, or rather with tiny, biting ice crystals driven along on a wind that picked up momentum swiftly—a wind that chilled more with each passing moment.

I thought of Dolly, driving the fifty miles to Arriola. Ches's voice broke into my thoughts, "This is going to be a bad one, Rob. Maybe we ought to hurry a little."

Pa didn't answer, but he touched his horse lightly with his spurs. I could tell that he was beginning to chill. Driving snow was soaking his shirt, melting from the warmth of his body. The wind tugged at his hat, whipped his horse's tail forward between its legs. Growing ever stronger, the wind assumed a high, whining note. Then the land was blotted out, hidden behind a thick, driving curtain of snow.

I was suddenly frantic with fear for Dolly. I was familiar with that road to Arriola, knew it was treacherous when the visibility was bad. She had a good team, but any team would drift a little with a wind as strong as this. On that road, a two-foot drift to one side meant an overturned buckboard, and Dolly dumped to freeze in a dry wash somewhere.

I spurred my horse up alongside of Pa and reaching over, grabbed his bridle and hauled him to a halt. I thought he was going to strike me, but he didn't. I said, "Damn you, use your head! You want Dolly hurt and maybe froze to death? You can't turn the Owens bunch out in this anyway. They'd never make it to town."

I'd never seen him so furious. I flinched at the impact of his eyes, but I couldn't let my own gaze waver. Pa was shivering violently, whether from cold or temper I couldn't tell. Behind us the crew bunched, crowding, thoroughly bewildered.

Glaring at me, Pa shouted over the rising noise of wind, "You came along to stop me, didn't you?"

I nodded.

"What would you have done if the storm hadn't come up?" I could see his teeth, bared as he drew breath into his lungs.

I shook my head, not knowing the answer. I'd only known my determination to stop him. Fate seemed to have intervened in the form of this storm, postponing the problem but not eliminating it.

I thought I understood my premonition of disaster now. It involved Dolly. Dolly, I was sure, would not be found in time.

Pa persisted, "What would you have done?"

Suddenly I lost my temper. He was wasting precious time while Dolly fought the storm alone. I yelled hysterically, "Damn you, maybe I'd have blown your head off! You satisfied now?"

I hated him then more than I ever had before. For an instant his fury blazed at me, and then it was gone. He wheeled his horse. "Somebody give me a coat. The rest of you go on back. I'm going after Dolly."

He took a sheepskin from the half-dozen offered, and shrugged into it. Then, wheeling his horse, he was gone into the storm.

Ches yelled, "Wait! I'm going too. A man hadn't ought to be alone in a storm like this." Ches took off after Pa. I sat motionless, thinking that since I was this close to the Owens place I might as well go on and give them the warning I felt I owed them. The crew turned away from me, heading into the wind. They hunched over in their saddles, burrowing into the collars of their sheepskin for protection from the biting wind. I faced it while I watched them go, and it snatched the breath greedily from my nostrils. I gasped, choking for air.

When they had disappeared, like ghostly, formless wraiths into the storm, I wheeled and continued toward the Owens place. My horse traveled willingly with the wind, and in a little more than half an hour, I saw the gray blob of the shack before me.

I rode my horse around behind it, so he'd have shelter from the wind. I dropped the reins and fought my way around to the front door. It flew open at my second knock and I stumbled inside.

Dave Owens and his two sons stood together, guns pointing at my midsection. A single oil lamp burned on the table, throwing off feeble rays of yellow light.

I said, "Not today. He was heading here but the snow

stopped him. He hasn't changed his mind, though. You can look for him again as soon as this storm clears."

They were suspicious of me. Dave Owens crossed to the window, scrubbed away the steam and peered outside. Turning, he looked at me sourly, "How come you go against your own Pa?" He looked at Lillie, standing frightened in a corner, then back at me.

I knew what he was thinking. And suddenly I knew that I had been building a mild pity for Lillie into something stronger simply because I didn't want to face the fact that I'd lost Rose.

I said sourly, "It's nothing new. I was doing it a long time before you came along."

I looked at the five of them, all scared and defiant, and yet possessed of a certain dignity too. I became aware that they were symbolic of the new race which was destined to people the Territory just as Pa was symbolic of the old, whose day was now nearly done.

Perhaps Pa would drive away this family, in spite of all I could do. But there would be more, by the thousands, until their very numbers overwhelmed him. It was their destiny to take the land from Pa, as it had been his destiny twenty years ago to take it from the Indians.

Lillie's enormous eyes made me uncomfortable. I pulled my collar up around my ears and tugged my hat down over my eyes. I had the feeling that I was looking at men already doomed to die.

I repeated inanely, "Watch for him when the storm clears," and turned toward the door, suddenly anxious to be outside, away from Lillie's mute plea, away from the atmosphere of hopeless, tenacious courage.

I yanked open the door and fought my way out into the wind. Riding into the teeth of the storm I remember being wildly angry because Pa was sacrificing everything to a cause already lost.

Chapter Seventeen

FROM CHES'S delirious babblings after he got back to K Diamond, I put together what had happened after he and Pa left. I did some guessing, too, but I think I came up with a substantially correct idea of what went on. . . .

For a while they rode almost directly into the wind, striking toward the road that ran between K Diamond and Arriola. Ches barely managed to keep Pa in sight.

They were almost blind, riding into the choking snow. Ches said he'd wondered if Pa wouldn't miss the road when he did reach it, but he needn't have worried about that. Pa knew every inch of K Diamond, in snow, in rain, in utter darkness. He wouldn't have missed the road.

As the storm grew worse, Pa became more frantic. It was apparent to Wolfe and probably to Pa as well that this was the worst storm K Diamond had ever been struck with. And as Pa became worried, he became more savagely determined, more reckless. He raked his horse's sides with his spurs until the animal, in sheer frenzy, reached a pace which would have been risky even on dry ground.

I knew that roan. He was a tremendous horse, with a heart as big as they came. He'd kill himself if Pa demanded it, and Pa demanded it that day.

Over dry washes, snow-filled almost to their brims, they sailed. Half a dozen times Ches yelled, "Slow down, you fool! Slow down!" but Pa paid him no heed.

Ches thought of Dolly, alone, frightened, cold, perhaps even lost by now. He thought of her, and of the team that would naturally drift, sideways a little, thus putting the buckboard in danger of dropping a wheel into some road-side washout.

Ches was chilled clear through. The temperature had plummeted swiftly, and now stood well below the zero mark. And still dropping. The air stayed choked with snow, and the ground was white except for the high spots where the wind kept it scoured clean.

They blundered into the midst of a bunch of K Diamond cattle, and the cattle spooked away, stopped, then stared at the pair with dumb eyes. Drifting already, Ches realized, and the storm had hardly started. Animals can gauge the severity of a storm as well as being able to tell when one is coming. Their early drift should have been a tipoff to both Ches and Pa. But both were too worried and concerned about Dolly to give it any thought.

Miles flowed beneath their straining horses. Sweat coated the horses' bodies, ice filled their nostrils. The cold, insistent and deadly, seeped through Ches's clothes, turning his legs and arms numb. He wondered how Dolly was faring. Much worse, he realized.

Since Ches's horse was neither as big nor as strong as Pa's roan, it was inevitable that Ches dropped behind. But still he followed, at times seeing the roan's tracks;

and when he lost them he followed by instinct, or by sounds which came downwind to him.

He never knew for sure just when he lost Pa. But when he did become sure, he stopped, and listened intently though the screaming wind made listening difficult.

He thought he heard a shout, and after that, the sound of a horse struggling on the ground. He tried to tell himself that the sounds were his imagination, born of his worry.

Later he blamed himself because he had not heeded his inner surety that Pa had met with an accident. He blamed himself because he hadn't spent more time in the search. He accused himself because out of anger at Pa and Pa's stubbornness, he didn't consider finding Pa as important as finding Dolly.

I can imagine how he justified his leaving the spot without making a thorough search of it, probably thinking he couldn't waste half the day poking around looking for him when he might not be down at all. He had to find Dolly.

It was the uncertainty that decided him, so he went on, leaving Pa on the ground, as we learned later, unconscious from hitting his head on a rock as he fell. Ches pointed his horse north again toward the Arriola road.

The wind whipped him savagely and the snow blinded him. He had to fight his horse every moment of the time, for the horse wanted only to turn and put that vicious wind at his back.

Ches passed the road, and only a vague memory of the horse stumbling in a wheel rut turned him back. He located it, and turned toward Arriola, urging his horse to a fast trot and shielding the upwind side of his face with the frozen collar of his sheepskin coat.

A nightmare of dragging hours followed for Ches. There were times when he knew he was on a hopeless quest, knew that Dolly could not possibly have lived this long. There were times when he was sure he would perish himself long before he found her. He kept on, and his guilt over leaving the place where he'd first missed Pa increased.

Sometimes, when the numbness in his legs and arms became frightening, he'd get down and walk painfully until circulation was restored. He could see less than ten feet ahead, ten feet to each side, and walking, had to be careful he didn't blunder clear off the road.

A year or so before, the K Diamond crew had built a bridge across a particularly deep bog where the road was perpetually washing out, and it was just beyond this bridge that Ches found the buckboard.

His horse saw it first and halted. Immediately out of the gloom ahead came the shrill nicker of another horse. And then Ches saw the rig and its empty seat.

Ches swung down from his horse. His stiffened legs would not support him and he fell, spread-eagled in the snow. He cursed savagely and clawed up the buckboard wheel until he was standing again. He pawed around in the snow-filled back of the rig, but he did not find Dolly. He shouted her name, his voice a panicked scream, for now he was sure he had left Pa behind, or Pa would have reached here first.

A vague instinct of self-preservation made him stamp his feet and fling his arms about his body to restore their circulation. He looked ahead at the horses and saw that one of them was standing, the other down.

He left the side of the buckboard and walked to the down horse. He knelt, examined one of the horse's legs, and the horse began to kick again.

Ches clawed back his coat. He drew his revolver and, moving around to the horse's head, thumbed back the hammer. He put a bullet between the animal's eyes and the shot made a flat, sharp sound in the snow-choked air. The other horse lunged away, but Ches snatched at its bridle and calmed him with a stroking hand and a gentle voice.

It was plain to Ches now what had happened. Dolly, probably chilled and thoroughly terrified, had been hurrying. The horses had hit the slick plank bridge, and one of them had either fallen or put his foot through a rotting plank, thus breaking his leg.

And Dolly, not even having a gun with which to put the animal out of his misery, had gone on afoot.

Ches realized that he was sobbing. A lassitude, which should have told him he was slowly freezing to death, came over him, robbing him of his will to fight. Guilt over leaving Pa and his sorrow over Dolly both added to his unwillingness to make the effort necessary to get back to K Diamond.

He fished in his pocket for his knife. He'd cut this one horse free of the harness and let him go. He'd unsaddle his own horse and release him too. Somewhere the horses would find shelter and perhaps would live. But Ches would stay here, and sleep.

His hands were numb with the cold. But he found his knife and withdrew it from his pocket. He couldn't hang onto it and it dropped into the snow.

He got to his knees and searched for it, but he couldn't find it and its loss assumed an exaggerated importance in his mind. He began to dig in the snow.

And then, an odd sound intruded into his consciousness. A whimpering sound. A woman crying.

Instantly the knife and its odd importance was forgotten. He lunged to his feet and heard that sound again, and went searching.

And suddenly Dolly was in his arms, sobbing, "Rob! Oh Rob! I prayed that you'd come. I—" She drew away, knowing almost as soon as she touched him that this was not Rob.

Ches shouted, "Where were you? I thought you were dead."

She pointed at the bridge. "I got under the bridge and crouched against the bank. The wind is broken there."

There was a question in her eyes which Ches could not meet. Abruptly he turned away. "I'll get the harness off this horse. I'll put my saddle horse in his place."

Cold as they were, his hands found the buckles in the harness by instinct. He pulled the harness from under the body of the dead horse and took bridle and collar off him. Then he backed the horse that was left until there was room to lead his saddle horse in.

He caught his horse, standing a few feet away. He

unsaddled and automatically flung saddle, blanket and bridle into the back of the buckboard. Ten minutes later he again had a team in harness.

He helped Dolly up onto the seat. Her face was frightened, and in his guilt, Ches thought it was accusing too. She shouted above the wind, "Where is Rob, Ches?"

"I lost him!" he called back at her. "We got separated in the storm!"

"Lost him? How?"

"His horse was faster than mine. He pulled away from me." He couldn't meet her eyes.

Dolly's eyes were filled with despair. For she knew, just as Ches knew, that Rob was down somewhere in the storm, or he'd have arrived here first.

Ches turned the team, threaded slowly across the bridge, and foot by foot, began the long journey home.

Somewhere along the way, his reason became deranged, so that when he reached K Diamond with Dolly, he was raving with delirium. . . .

Chapter Eighteen

I DON'T KNOW what I expected to accomplish by following the same general direction in which Pa and Ches had gone, instead of heading toward K Diamond. I had some vague idea that I might find Dolly even if the two of them failed, and that perhaps by so doing would gain stature in Pa's eyes.

I experienced the same difficulty which Pa and Ches had in forcing my horse to travel into the wind. I spurred mercilessly until my spur rowels were bright with blood, for the animal fought with stubborn tenacity to get his head out of the wind.

Any sense of direction is lost in a blizzard such as this one. Today, however, I had the wind to guide me, the steady north wind. To ride into it was to ride toward K Diamond. I put it on my left quarter and so headed toward a point where I guessed Dolly might possibly be intercepted.

Normally, the Owens place was a little more than two hours from K Diamond. Today, however, fighting every inch of the way against snow and wind, I guessed it would take four—maybe four and a half hours to reach the point on the Arriola road toward which I was headed.

I knew a mounting fear as I traveled, for I had never experienced such a storm as this. The cold was intense— I guessed the temperature at close to twenty below—with a forty-mile wind blowing.

I turned the collar of my sheepskin up and buttoned it so that only my eyes showed above it. I tied my bandanna over my head and under my chin and crammed my hat down atop that, and these things helped keep my face from freezing.

Time ceased to have meaning. It was as though I had spent my life riding against this savage wind, on a treadmill which kept me from making any forward progress. Somewhere during the ride I lost all hope of finding Dolly alive. I even began to lose hope of reaching K Diamond alive myself.

The light had faded to a weird half-light where nothing

had any color, but in which everything seemed made up of varying shades of gray and white. I don't know how long I traveled. But it must have been late in the afternoon when the blob of darker gray ahead caught my eye—a moving shape that I first took for a cow.

Almost immediately I realized it was taller than a cow. It must be a horse.

Without thought I reined over to intercept it, recognizing its shape even at this distance and in this poor light. I realized it was saddled even though I saw no distinct saddle outline. As soon as I had approached to within twenty feet, I recognized Pa's big roan.

Panic hit me with a shock. I spurred my horse recklessly and leaning over, caught up the roan's reins, one of which was broken. He didn't want to turn back into the wind. I thought I'd break the single bridle rein and pull my arm out of its socket trying to turn him. Finally, in desperation, I looped the rein around my saddlehorn, and with a whispered hope that it would hold, set spurs to my own horse.

I turned the roan and dragged him along behind. No use trying to find tracks, I knew—they were completely drifted over. But I reasoned that Pa's horse would have been drifting with the wind, and that by heading directly into it, I could approximate the trail he had followed. Pa was down somewhere in the snow, perhaps hurt. And if Pa was down, it was unlikely that Dolly had been found. And where was Ches?

I got down off my own horse and examined the roan; trying to figure from the frozen sweat on his hide, from the snow and ice caked on his rump, from the ice in the saddle, how long he had been without a rider. I guessed somewhere close to half an hour. I guessed too, that I would travel almost as fast upwind as the horse had drifted downwind.

I turned directly into the wind. I rode for what seemed like half an hour and then stopped. I fumbled at the flap of my coat for nearly ten minutes before I managed to get my gun out. It must have taken another couple of minutes before I could get the hammer thumbed back. I fired and waited, listening, but I heard nothing save for the scream of the wind as it broke against my body and those of the horses.

I went on, pausing and firing and listening at intervals of about ten minutes.

At last my gun was empty save for one last load. I still carried the old Dance Brothers and Park percussion revolver, but I knew that reloading it was out of the question in this cold. Reloading one of the newer, cartridge models would have been almost more than a man could manage.

With one load left, I debated as to whether I should use it now or wait. I stretched the interval between it and the last shot to about twenty minutes, and at last raised the gun and fired.

I listened with painful intentness.

I almost missed it, so faintly did it come to my ears. It might have been the sharp sound of a horse's hoof striking a half-covered rock. Only by its direction did I recognize it for a shot.

It seemed to come from off to my right and ahead, and at once I spurred my horse in that direction. I had begun to think I'd missed him, when a second shot banged out immediately before me.

Still I could see nothing, so I raised my voice and bellowed, "Pa! Is that you? Sing out, so I can locate you!"

My horses were still moving and all at once I was right on top of him. He was standing spraddle-legged, to keep the wind from blowing him off his feet.

I swung down, without turning loose of either horse's reins. Pa's head was bare and there was a wild, blank look in his eyes. My legs were so cold and numb that I had difficulty in standing myself. I yelled, "Where's Ches?"

He shook his head. Then I saw the blood that ran from a gash in his head and down across his cheek. It was partly dried; but there was a new, fresh trickle through the dried old blood which indicated that the wound was still bleeding.

Pa seemed dazed and unable to think for himself. I shouted, "I found your horse! Mount up and we'll head on home!"

His lips made a word that sounded like "Dolly," but I gave him no encouragement. If his life were to be saved, I knew he had to be got home to K Diamond at once. He tried to mount and fell to the ground. Still holding both horses like grim death, I helped him to his feet and then helped him mount. I'd no more than got him settled when another sound intruded and another shape materialized out of the driving snow.

Another one who had lost his horse, probably attracted to this spot by the sound of Pa's shots. I assumed it was Ches, and was therefore startled when he came close and I recognized Dell Anson.

Recognizing me at the same instant, he started and leaped away. He clawed frantically at the flap of his coat.

I couldn't move. I had no loads in my gun anyway. Pa's gun must have dropped from his hand, for he no longer held it and I was sure he couldn't have returned it to its holster.

I had the most insane desire to laugh. We were fighting for life in this damned storm, and now here was Dell Anson materializing out of it to try and cheat the storm of us.

The desire to laugh grew in me, and I know it was mostly hysteria. Dell moved as though half asleep, but he didn't seem to be aware of his own slowness. He was so completely numbed by cold that his body simply wouldn't respond any more.

He clawed up the coat flap, but it was stiff and awkward, and fell back again. He tried a second time, and failed again. He began to fumble at the buttons of his coat so that he could throw it back and draw. His numbed fingers couldn't get even one button undone.

I did laugh then. I laughed like a crazy man, and the laughter warmed me and made the blood pound again through my body. Hell, Dell Anson could stand here trying all day and never get his gun out. And even if he did get it out, he'd never be able to thumb back the hammer. His gun was of no more use to him than my empty one was to me.

I turned my back on Dell, turned to see how Pa was taking this. He seemed disinterested, unconcerned. He'd lost his will with his strength apparently, but whether this was caused by the cold or by his head injury, I couldn't tell. I put his reins in his hand and wound the ends around his wrist so he wouldn't lose them.

I put my hand on my own saddlehorn and started to mount, then realized suddenly that I had forgotten Dell. I paused and looked at him across my horse's back.

He had stopped trying to get out his gun. He was just standing there looking at me. In reversed circumstances he'd have abandoned me and he was expecting me now to abandon him.

For a moment I was tempted. I thought of Rose, who might be mine if I left Dell here. I tried briefly to justify my thoughts with the fact that Dell had just tried to kill me.

I was instantly ashamed. I yelled, "Come on, damn it! Climb up. I'll ride behind you." There was a good reason why I wanted to be behind him. It would be harder for him to push me off the horse if I were behind.

He made three tries before he managed to mount and I didn't get close enough to help him. He tried to kick the horse into motion but I still held the reins. Wary of his left boot, I put a foot into the stirrup and swung awkwardly up behind him.

Pa didn't have what it took to force his horse into the wind, so I slipped my lariat loop around the animal's head, dallied the rope to my saddlehorn, and moved out, trailing the roan behind.

An eternity began, during which the light faded to dark. But at last we struck the road, and turned into it, and a little while later met a bunch of K Diamond punchers searching for us.

I could relax in the saddle at last, for they took our reins and trailed our horses behind theirs at a punishing trot all the way home to K Diamond.

I know that Pa was nearly unconscious, but he managed to stay in his saddle without help, although he apparently did not hear the punchers' talk as they rode along. I was glad he didn't because it was talk about Dolly and Ches—still missing, and believed dead.

I came out of my numbed stupor long enough to order half a dozen of the K Diamond hands to leave us and ride along the Arriola road, where I hoped they still might find Ches and Dolly alive.

They grumbled, fearful of the storm and cold, but they finally went, and with those that were left we eventually reached K Diamond in night's first pitch-blackness.

They wrapped us in blankets and kept us away from the warmest rooms. I dropped off to sleep before they had even laid me down on my bed.

I awoke about an hour later in the most excruciating pain I have ever experienced. Blood was flowing again into my frostbitten legs and arms. I lay there sweating, gritting my teeth, swearing under my breath until I could stand motionlessness no longer. Then I got up, not even noticing that I was still fully dressed, and paced back and forth from wall to wall. I chewed my lip until the blood ran. I clawed at my hair until my scalp felt raw. And I clenched my fists until they were numb.

Out in the living room I could hear someone talking. Without bothering with my boots, I went out.

It was Ches, and he was alone in the room, lying on a horsehair sofa talking to himself. I listened, because it took my mind from the maddening pain in my arms and legs, hands and feet. I paced up and down and listened, and learned from his delirious ravings what had happened after he and Pa had left the rest of us early this morning.

As I paced up and down I became aware that someone else had entered the room, and glancing around I saw Pa.

His head was bandaged, I supposed for the gash in his scalp. Later I found out his ears had been badly frostbitten, so much so that he eventually lost the tips of them both.

He must have been in as much pain as I—perhaps more. But it was not physical pain which I saw in his face. It was mental anguish, and seeing it, I realized he had heard just enough of Ches's ravings to form an entirely erroneous idea of what had happened. He thought Ches had deliberately abandoned him to die.

He started toward Ches, his eyes crazy, but I stepped between them. "Stay away from him. The poor bastard's still out of his head."

"Get out of my way." His voice had a strange, cold quality.

I didn't move. I was past being scared of him. Right

then I could feel only hate, and perhaps it gave me more courage than I usually had. I said, "Ches didn't deliberately leave you. He lost you in the storm. You pulled ahead of him. He had a hunch you were down, that's all. He blames himself because he didn't search long enough, but he was thinking of Dolly."

His eyes didn't change. They were wild and not quite rational. They didn't seem to see me at all, but looked beyond and through me. I realized that Pa, as well as Ches, was partly out of his head. He'd made up his mind that Ches had tried to kill him and now he was going to retaliate.

He tried to fling me aside. I couldn't believe that even Pa could do what he obviously intended to do, which was to kill Ches with his bare hands. Then I stepped back and swung my right fist as hard as I could.

Its sound, connecting with his jutting jaw, was like the meaty smack of a bullet striking a deer. His head snapped back and he tottered. He took a backward step, crouched a little and raised his fisted hands to defend himself. But I didn't move and his eyes cleared a little of their wildness. He looked at me, seeming to see me clearly for the first time. "Jeff! What the hell's going on?"

He dropped his hands as though wondering why they were clenched and raised, and shook his massive head. One of his hands went up and pulled at his great, tawny mustache. I was ashamed of hitting him, but I couldn't drown the rebellious defiance that burned like a slow fire within me.

I said, my voice sounding cold, "You were going to kill

Ches, because you thought that out in the storm he abandoned you to die. He didn't, but God damn it, I wouldn't have blamed him if he had. You rode him all morning, accusing him of being in love with Dolly. You ride everybody until you force them to turn on you. You think you're mighty as God, but you're not. You're only a backwoods cattle baron who's riding for a fall. Dell Anson tried to kill both you and me out there in the storm. When he comes to, he'll try again. Owens hates you, and even I hate you."

He seemed surprised. "Why?"

I laughed bitterly. "Why? You ought to know. You have to own everything. You had to buy Dell Anson's trial and when you did you finished me for practicing law in Arriola. Do you think there's anyone in Arriola county that would hire me now? You had to buy the sheriff the day we buried Manuel. It's either gold or bullets with you, isn't it? But neither gold nor bullets would buy Dolly, so you lost her. Maybe some day you'll realize that gold and bullets aren't enough."

His mouth had twisted at my mention of Dolly and his eyes turned bleak. His hand swung viciously and connected hard with my cheek. My head snapped aside. He spoke to me as though I were still a small boy, "Don't use that tone on me, bucko!"

I turned my back and walked over to the fire.

My arms and legs ached dully now, the worst of the pain gone. I moved my fingers and toes experimentally and decided that no permanent damage had been done to them. The outside door opened, letting in a swirl of driven snow that blew halfway across the room before the door was slammed. One of the crewmen stood there looking at Pa, choking for breath which had been snatched from him by the wind in the short distance between bunkhouse and ranch house.

He said, "Dell Anson's coming out of it, boss. He's doin' some talkin'. Figures to kill you an' Jeff here. You want us to tie him up 'till the storm lets up an' we can haul him to the sheriff in Arriola?"

Pa said evenly, "Get the hell out of here."

"But what about Dell?"

"Just leave him be."

The man shrugged. He looked at me in a puzzled way, then shook his head and went back outside. Before the door closed he seized a rope that had been strung between the house and the bunkhouse.

I went over to close the door for him. He nodded at me and disappeared into the driving snow, traveling hand over hand along the rope.

When I turned, Pa was watching me. I asked, "Why the hell did you tell him that? Dell will be coming to the house with a gun in his hand the first time he gets a chance."

"Let him come."

"So you can kill him, I suppose?"

He wouldn't bait. He studied me for a moment, an inscrutable expression on his face. But his eyes looked like those of a hurt animal. That went way and he grinned at me mirthlessly, "I ain't the only one Dell's after."

I could feel my anger rising again because I felt the

need to defend my own conduct to him. I said, "You ought to know me better than that, I was only over there once and I never got closer to Rose than ten feet. Jim Purser wouldn't have fed those stories to Dell, either, if he hadn't wanted to get back at you for fencing him off."

He shrugged, but he kept grinning at me and I knew he thought I was lying. He thought I'd been carrying on with Rose and was denying it now because I didn't want to face the consequences.

I fished in my pocket for makings and rolled myself a smoke. I remember wondering where Pa and I had forked away from the single road we both had traveled at first to the separate ones we now traveled. I wondered where it would lead, where it would end.

My feeling of foreboding came back and I was suddenly very sure of one thing, which was that one or more of us would be dead before it was ended. One or more of us wouldn't see the sun shining out of a clear sky again. When the blizzard ended there would also be lives that were ended here at K Diamond.

Chapter Nineteen

THE MORE I THOUGHT of Dell Anson, the more uneasy I got. Maybe my fear was more of killing Dell than of being killed myself, but I suppose it was a combination of the two. In any case, Rose was lost to me. Just thinking of her still had the power to stir me, and I guessed it always would. I wonder why a man never quite realizes the value of something until it's lost to him.

I knew that I had to talk to Dell before he found a gun and came to the house looking for Pa and me.

Ches had gone back to sleep, and Pa was sitting silently before the fire, staring into the flames. I went to my room and pulled on my boots. I got my sheepskin and put it on, then I went outside and fought my way along the guide rope.

Although it was dark, I knew there were lights in the bunkhouse. I watched for them, but I had traveled more than half the short distance between the two buildings before I saw them, the snow was so thick. It was bitterly cold. I didn't see how so much snow could fall, as cold as it was. I was chilled all the way through by the time I reached the bunkhouse and flung open the door.

A poker game, seven-handed, was going on at the table around the single lamp. Several of the men stretched out idly on their bunks. Dell was by himself in a lower bunk at the back of the room. His eyes were open and he was staring at the ceiling.

I hated to talk in front of the crew, but I didn't see any other way. I pulled a straight-backed chair over close to his bunk and sat down straddling it, my arms resting on its back.

Now that I was here, I didn't know what to say. He kept staring at the ceiling, refusing to look at me, but his face slowly flushed and I knew he was aware of my presence. I asked finally, "Why did you try to kill me, Dell?"

He looked at me, and for a moment I thought he'd spring out of the bunk at me. His eyes were filled with a crazy hatred.

I asked, "Do you blame me because Pa bought that trial?"

He shook his head.

"Then it's Rose?"

I could see the muscles in his body tighten. His face twisted. I said quickly, "Dell, I went over there just once. I felt it was my fault I lost your case in court and that I owed it to you to see that Rose was all right. Purser happened to ride in as I was leaving."

His eyes called me a liar. I began to feel my own anger rising. I said, "You know, don't you, that by accusing me you're also accusing her? I'll tell you something. I'd like to have ridden over there every day. But I didn't because Rose told me not to come again."

He swung in the bunk so fast it startled me. His feet struck the back of the chair on which I was sitting and toppled me backward to the floor. I had scarcely struck when he was on me. An elbow caught me in the mouth, a knee in the groin. Rising, he grabbed the chair in his hands and brought it smashing down on my head.

But I kept coming up. I was mad by then, mad clear through. The crew halted their game and one of them seized the lamp and retreated to the far wall. Others were moving the table out of the way. I had a quick glance at their faces as I struggled upward, and what I saw surprised me. They wanted to see me whipped, every one of them. They believed, as Dell did, that I was guilty of playing around with Dell's wife.

The realization that they did fanned my anger. Dell swung the smashed chair which he still held in his hands, and one of its legs cracked savagely against my tender left ear.

Pain removed all restraint from me. If he wanted a fight I'd give it to him! He'd had me at a disadvantage so far, but I'd change that.

I retreated halfway across the room before I got set. Then as he came rushing at me, I straightened him up with a right that smashed his lips against his teeth. He rocked back, steadied, and spat blood. His eyes were murderous. He was a little shorter than I, but just as heavy. And his muscles were like steel from the prison rockpile.

He was the outraged husband, and his fighting showed it. I was mad, but I didn't have the impetus to make me want to kill that he did. I suppose that's what made it so uneven those first few minutes.

He drove me back, throwing blows that fell like rain in my face and chest. I kept trying to get set again, but he kept me off balance until at last the wall was at my back. Then he seemed to think he had me whipped. He came in carelessly, wanting to knock me down. He must have known that the crew wouldn't stand by and let him kill me, but he sure intended to try. And he had to get me down before he could.

I threw myself forward, aiming a right that I brought up from my side at his jaw. It didn't connect with his jaw, but struck him full in the throat.

His head snapped back, and he gagged and choked. Both his hands came up to claw at his throat, and I hit him again, this time flush on the forehead.

That one snapped his head back with an audible crack.

Now it was my turn and I didn't let it pass. I followed him, driving hard, savage blows at his belly when his hands were up, at his unprotected face when they were down. I drove him back across the room as he had driven me, by furious, cutting blows that left marks everywhere they struck.

I drove him back against the far wall and still I pounded him, until his eyes glazed and he slipped down the wall to the floor. I lost my head. I was fighting by instinct, by fury, and when he went to the floor I went with him.

The crew dragged me off. I heard the babble of their voices over the dull roaring in my head, "Jeff, don't kill him." "Jeff, that's enough! He's whipped!"

I was panting harshly, trembling. Reality came back to me slowly and my muscles relaxed. Dell lay beaten and bleeding on the floor, conscious, but only barely so.

Somewhere, someone muttered, "By God! Take his wife and then beat him to hell!"

I swung around. "Whoever said that can draw his time—and get the hell out as soon as this storm clears."

The faces of them all were hard and unfriendly. The worst of it was, I couldn't blame them. Dell Anson had been hurt too much by K Diamond already. And there was no use in my denying that I had been chasing Rose. A denial would change none of their minds. I scowled and pulled my torn sheepskin around me. I stalked to the door and slammed angrily out into the screaming wind.

I stood on the snow-covered, narrow gallery trembling like a kid. My breath dragged in and out harshly, and the bitter cold seemed to freeze my lungs with each breath.

I was sweating, and the wind chilled my sweated body in seconds. I began to shiver violently.

I grabbed the rope and pulled myself hand over hand to the house. I went in and Pa swung his massive head to look at me. "What happened to you?"

"Fight with Dell Anson. I tried to tell him I hadn't been seeing Rose. But he's crazy. You'd better have him locked up until you can haul him into town. He'll get a gun somewhere if you don't."

Pa laughed, a strange laugh that was harsh and uncaring. "Let the bastard get a dozen guns."

I shrugged. Pa was a stranger to me today. Whatever warmth he'd had before was gone altogether.

Over on the sofa, Ches groaned and stirred.

I said, "You'll never change, will you? The whole damned world can change but you never will. Face it, Pa—the old days of free range are gone. You can't hold K Diamond even if you kill Owens. There's thousands like Owens and you can't kill them all."

He kept on looking at me in that brooding way that was almost frightening. He spoke, his voice low-pitched, intense. "I swore nobody would ever take anything away from me again. Not land, nor water, nor cattle. They won't, either."

I said, "I'm leaving K Diamond, Pa. I can't leave as long as Dell Anson thinks he wants to kill me, and I won't until this business about the Owens family is settled. But I'll leave as soon as those two things are settled, and I don't plan to come back."

Anger touched his eyes, and then his lip curled. "What am I supposed to do, shed tears? Go any time you damn please."

"All right, Pa."

There didn't seem to be anything else to say, but for a moment I didn't turn away. I kept watching him.

He'd never shown me any particular affection, but there had been a closeness between us during the time we were traveling west together, and later while we built K Diamond. I wondered whether the change had been in Pa or in myself.

I couldn't help feeling a little sorry for him. The empire was crumbling. Signs of its disintegration were written everywhere. He was losing Dolly and myself. Remaining was the crew, and he had nothing from them but the loyalty they were paid for, and I wondered if he had even this from them all. I recalled the way they'd looked at me during my fight with Dell.

Suddenly Pa flushed darkly, and I realized I had been staring at him. He looked up and his eyes flashed their old blue flame. "Get out of here!" he said. His voice was low, his lips barely moved. But a chill ran through my body at the tone of his voice.

I turned and walked away. I went down the hall to my room and once inside I lighted the lamp.

I could hear the scream of the wind against the house, higher and fiercer, if anything, than it had been before. I slipped off my coat and boots and lay down on the bed, intending to rest only a moment.

But I fell asleep instantly, and did not wake again until

late morning of the following day.

The wind still screamed against the house. In the yard, drifts were piled behind each windbreak, and some of them looked four or five feet deep. The air was filled with blowing snow, but whether it was new snow or snow picked up from the ground, I couldn't tell.

As I watched, a bunch of cattle drifted into the yard. Ice crusted their faces, mouths and nostrils. Ice was a thick coat on their backs and rumps. They traveled weakly, listlessly.

One of them, a yearling steer, stumbled and fell not fifty feet from the house. He kicked a couple of times and then lay still. I watched with dumb fascination as the bellows of his breathing slowed and finally stopped. He hadn't even stopped breathing before the snow began to drift up behind him, and I knew that within a few minutes he would be covered over.

Was this happening on the whole range? Or was this only a bunch of weak ones? A yearling steer shouldn't be weak, I thought, and that one hadn't looked thin or weak.

I pulled on my boots and went out into the hall. From there I could see Pa, staring into the fireplace as though he hadn't moved all night. Ches was gone—to the bunkhouse probably. Dolly was standing at the window, her shoulders slumped dispiritedly. As I came into the room, Franklin, the cook, came in from the kitchen with tray and cups and a steaming pot of coffee.

He set the tray down on the table and poured three cups full. Dolly turned from the window and gave me a wan smile. "Good morning, Jeff."

"Morning."

Pa moved his head slightly, but he didn't turn. I said, "A yearling steer just died in the yard."

That brought him out of his chair. He glanced at me briefly, then grabbed his coat from the sofa beside him and slammed outside. Dolly sipped her coffee listlessly. "I saw it. It was horrible. What will become of all those poor beasts if this storm doesn't stop?"

I said, "They'll die, like that steer did. Might have been something the matter with him—maybe he was weak, or sick, or something. But if it keeps up another day, there'll be a lot of losses."

"The Owens family—will they be all right?"

"Probably."

She studied me for a few moments. Her face was pale, and there were dark circles beneath her eyes. She was a changed woman from the Dolly I remembered. I asked, "No ill effects from the cold?"

"No, Jeff. Not in my body at least." She glanced hastily at the door, then back at me. "Jeff, you've got to tell me. What's happened between Rob and Ches?"

I tried to evade, but I couldn't. Her eyes begged too hard. I said, "Pa thinks Ches abandoned him to die out there in the storm. Ches blames himself because he didn't look hard enough after he missed Pa. But he was worried about you and he couldn't be sure Pa was down."

"Why should Rob think that when Ches has always been so loyal?"

"Maybe he can't face his own failure with you. So he's

made up his mind that Ches is in love with you."

Pa came banging into the house. He glanced at us, and I'm sure he knew we had been discussing him. But he seemed to have no thought for us, only for the cattle. "I've got to do something! That wasn't even one of my steers. It was Longstreet's. It drifted all the way from El Espalto de Cerdo."

I said, "Nothing you can do."

"The hell!" He banged out of the house again. I went over to the window and saw him fighting his way to the bunkhouse. After a while he came plunging back. He came in, panting heavily, and headed at once toward his bedroom. When he came out again, he was warmly dressed. There was a woolen scarf tied over his head and his hat atop it. He was pulling on a pair of heavy gloves and his feet were encased in boot galoshes.

Dolly gasped, "Rob! You're not going out in this?"

"Why not? I've got to see what's happening to the cattle." He looked at me and a small, sour grin touched his lips. "You can quit worryin' about Dell. He left at daybreak."

Dolly's voice was suddenly concerned. "You're not going after the Owenses?"

He stared at her coldly. "Not until the storm quits." He scowled and went outside, slamming the door viciously behind him.

I went over to the window and watched. My thoughts and feelings were confused. My first reaction at hearing Dell had left had been relief, for now his danger to us was gone. On the heels of that I felt a wild, uncontrollable jealousy. Dell had gone home to the badlands. Even now, at this very moment, Rose might be in his arms.

I cursed myself savagely. What right had I to be jealous of Dell? He was Rose's husband. He would be Rose's husband until he was dead.

I told myself that underneath I was just like Pa, greedy and possessive. I would fight as hard as he did to take the things I wanted, and to keep them after I got them. The main difference between Pa and myself lay in the simple fact that up to now I hadn't wanted anything badly enough to fight for it. K Diamond was an obsession to him, but it was much less than that to me.

I turned to Dolly. "How much different are we, Dolly? Would I do the things he does if I cared as much for K Diamond as he does?"

She probably meant to smile and give me a light answer. But something in my face must have stopped her. "I think you are very much like him, Jeff. I think if you had been subjected to the same stresses he has that you'd probably act exactly as he does."

Her words shocked me. I remembered the night before, and my fight with Dell in the bunkhouse. I'd tried to kill him—I knew that now. I'd tried to kill him because I'd wanted his wife. My own mind had betrayed me and I hadn't realized it at the time. But back there, deep in my subconscious, the desire had existed.

I said, speaking as though to myself, "How about the time I put a gun on that Mexican who had come after Pa for stealing his cattle? I couldn't pull the trigger. And how about the bunch of 'Paches? I couldn't shoot them either. I'd never have hanged Rolie and Clay Anson. I'm not like him!"

Dolly was too wise to argue. I said, too forcefully, "I believe in the law!"

"Yes," she said softly. "And perhaps that is the difference between you. The law failed to protect Rob, beginning that night when your mother was killed. So he feels a defiance toward it, and makes his own laws as he goes along."

I had turned back to the window as she spoke. Now I scrubbed frost from it and through the hole I'd made saw Pa and half a dozen of the crew ride out. Scarcely had they disappeared into the driving blizzard when I saw another figure riding in, riding hard as though the devil were in pursuit. . . .

She was so bulky with clothes that at first I failed to recognize her. But as she slid her sweated horse to a halt before the gallery, I caught a glimpse of her face, and at once my heart seemed to stop. The blood drained from my face and my hands turned to ice.

Then I was running toward the door. It flung open and she came in, driven by a gust of wind.

Rose! Oh my God, it was Rose!

She was covered with snow. Her face was red; her eyes held a torment of panicked fear. When she saw me they filled with tears.

Dolly was forgotten, and so was Dell. Rose came to my arms as though she belonged there. She gasped as I crushed her to me.

Then she struggled free. Self-consciously she stood,

her eyes averted, brushing snow from her clothes. "Jeff, he's coming after you! I thought he'd beat me here. He came home this morning—" She pulled off her stocking cap and her hair tumbled free around her shoulders. "Jeff, he was crazy. He accused me—you—"

"I know." I saw the marks of Dell's fists on her face now. One of her eyes had a blue-black circle beneath it, and one of her cheeks was cut. Her lips were puffy. I'd never known such rage as I felt at that moment.

The look on my face must have frightened her. She gave me one glance and then looked at the floor. She whispered, "He came home after his gun. He said he was going to kill both Rob and you. Then he was coming back to kill me. Jeff, he's clear out of his mind."

Dolly, who had remained quietly in the background, now came forward. I said, "Rose, this is Dolly."

"Rob's wife?" Rose asked.

Dolly said, "Yes. Come and get out of those heavy clothes. And let me do something about that cut on your face."

Rose looked at me as though she couldn't bear to leave me. I said, feigning a confidence I didn't feel, "Go ahead, Rose. Don't worry about Dell."

Little Lee came running toward me from the kitchen, brandishing two wooden guns in his chubby fists.

Maria, his Mexican nurse, followed, watching him fondly. I knelt and put my arms around him, and he gave me a childish hug. I said to Maria, "Keep him out of sight for a while. There may be some trouble. Is his room warm enough?"

179

"*Sí.*" She hustled him away, protesting and wailing.

I went back to the window. I tried to put myself in Dell's place, and to guess what he would do. He'd be cold when he rode in. His hands would be stiff. He'd want to get warm, before he started anything. Perhaps even now he was in one of the buildings at K Diamond, warming himself before a hastily built fire.

He was no longer the Dell Anson I'd known before. He was insane with fury at K Diamond's persecution. He'd been brooding up there at the pen for half a year, and then had heard the lies Purser told him about Rose and myself.

There would be no chance to talk to him. I'd tried that.

I considered the courses open to me. I could kill him on sight and the law would justify me. Dell was an escaped convict. He had made open threats to kill both Pa and myself. We knew he had a gun. Whatever happened, there'd be no trouble with the law over it.

But if my hand killed Dell, the killing would build an insurmountable wall between Rose and me. As if the one already there weren't high enough.

Rose's horse still stood near the house. I shrugged into my coat and went out. The wind blasted me so hard that I had to lean into it to stand. Staggering, slipping, I led the horse toward the barn.

I went into the barn leading Rose's horse, and the animal almost ran me down in his eagerness to get inside. I jumped out of the way, stumbled over a bin half full of oats, staggered and fell. It was all that saved me.

A rifle cracked sharply from the gloomy rear of the barn and the bullet tore a chunk of wood as big as my fist from an upright just behind me.

Rose's horse backed, laid back his ears and stood trembling, crouched on his haunches. I saw a rifle sticking out of the saddleboot as I scrambled on hands and knees across the littered floor toward a couple of hay bales.

The second rifle shot, hard on the heels of the first, kicked up a handful of straw and manure a foot ahead of me and almost blinded me.

This time the horse went wild. Perhaps the bullet nicked him, or perhaps it was only its thunder in such an enclosed space. He reared and began to buck toward me.

I didn't have much time for thinking, but I knew if the third rifle bullet didn't get me, the hoofs of that damned horse would. I flung myself up, and dived for the two hay bales.

Coming down, one of the horse's forefeet struck me in the back. It was a glancing blow but it hurt like hell as it raked the entire length of my back. With that for added impetus, I slammed forward, sprawled across the two hay bales and rolled behind them.

My back was on fire, and my lungs were begging for air. I lay there panting, listening as the horse bucked down the length of the barn. I longed for that rifle on his saddle, because my revolver was in the house.

There wasn't any doubt in my mind as to who the hidden rifleman was. It was Dell Anson. He'd done as I expected him to, had hidden here in the barn to warm his hands and limber them up. I thought about calling to him to tell him I was unarmed, but I wouldn't let him think I'd beg. Besides, I doubted if it would do any good. It would only make him come after me faster.

A horse collar lay nearby, a hole in it and the stuffing coming out. I picked it up and heaved it out into the alleyway, thinking that if I could lure Dell into another shot maybe the shot would chase that bucking horse back toward me. If that happened, maybe I could get that rifle out of the boot.

Dell didn't disappoint me. He must have been right on the ragged edge of firing anyway. Hardly had the horse collar struck than his rifle boomed.

Immediately Rose's horse, which had stopped bucking, began again, now heading back toward me. I poked my head out to look. Dell's rifle roared again and I pulled back, but not before I'd seen that rifle I wanted hanging half out of the boot, ready to fall at the next jump.

Almost as quickly as I'd pulled my head back, I poked it out again. The rifle was still hanging from the boot by no more than the front sight, and with the horse's every jump it bounded wildly upward and then descended to bang against his front legs.

I pulled my legs under me, and tensed to leap for it the instant the horse came abreast. But just as I leaped, the gun fell, and I sprawled in the open, rolled onto my back and flung up my hands to catch it.

Dell's next bullet burned along my shoulder as I caught the rifle, but I kept on rolling, working the lever as I did, and flung a wild, undirected shot at the rear of the barn. Without pausing, I came to my feet and dived back behind the hay bales.

Up to now, I'd acted more or less instinctively, driven

by the urgency of survival. Now, reaction to this sudden and unexpected peril set in. I began to shake. I told myself I was cold, but it was more than that. I faced a more formidable enemy than the scrawny Apache had been, and one just as savagely determined to kill.

But I believe in that instant I understood my father and the pressures that had driven him better than I ever had before. Where was protection from the law now? And how could I turn to it when it lay fifty miles away across a waste of screaming wind and driving snow?

There were times—and this was one of them—when a man made his own law or died.

The choice disgusted me. Kill Dell Anson or be killed myself. I didn't want it that way. Except for the marks his fists had put on Rose, I didn't hate Dell; and I didn't want to kill him.

Another choice occurred to me suddenly. I could run—or at least appear to run. With snow on the ground to track me in, Dell would be sure to follow. I could get a lead on him sufficient to put me out of his sight in the driving snow, and once I had him tracking me I could circle and come up behind him. Maybe I could surprise him and take him alive.

The more I thought about it, the more excited I became. I knew I hadn't much time left. Even now Dell might be up in the loft, edging along toward a place where he could fire down upon me from above.

I got my hand under the end of one of the hay bales and flipped it upward. It rolled out into the alleyway and came to rest in utter silence. Without further hesitation, and with a spot between my shoulder blades beginning to ache with the expectation of a bullet striking, I jumped to my feet and lunged for the door.

I almost made it. I was just going through when the rifle roared again, seemingly right in my ears, but actually almost over my head and up in the loft.

The bullet went right through my left ear, and it made no more impression on me than if I had grazed that ear against the door. There was no pain, but a sudden flow of blood soaked the side of my neck and ran down inside my shirt.

I left a splash of it in the white snow before the door, and then I was gone, stooping, running directly into the teeth of the storm. I slipped and floundered, but I kept driving; and that same spot between my shoulder blades began to ache again.

I ran until I thought I'd drop, trying to get enough lead to circle behind Dell before he'd read in my tracks what I intended to do.

Chapter Twenty

I WAS IN an eerie world of nothingness, seemingly bounded by the distance I could see, less than twenty feet. Snow stung my face and coated the front of me in minutes. I was lost in a void, and it was as though K Diamond were a million miles away. The wind chilled me to the bone in seconds. The blood from my ear froze as it dripped onto my coat collar, until it built up a small mound there of mingled blood and snow.

I heard no sound but the scream of wind, the noise of my boots striking the snow-covered, frozen ground.

I don't suppose I ran more than a hundred yards. Then I began to circle. I made what I judged to be a fifty-foot circle and then began to look for Dell's tracks as I came around toward my own trail.

This was the risky part. I could blunder right into him, never suspecting until it would be too late. I could come back into my trail ahead of him and get his bullet squarely in the back.

Panic washed over me and I wanted to turn and run. But I knew I couldn't. This was something that had to be faced—if not today, then some other time. I'd just as well face it now and have it done with.

The wind whipped the snow along the ground like a driving sheet, erasing tracks almost as fast as they were made. Another hazard. What if Dell lost my trail? What if I failed to find his?

I almost did exactly that. I crossed his partly obscured trail, seeing it only because of two footprints in a shallow drift that had remained longer than the others. I turned into the trail and began to run again, searching the white curtain ahead for a blacker shape that would be Dell Anson. At intervals I would pick up a few tracks swiftly vanishing into the snow that sifted over them.

Suddenly, coming downwind, I heard the sharp sound of a shot, a shot that must have been pointed directly into the wind, for it had an odd, flat sound.

So Dell was getting panicky. He was shooting at nothing, in the vain hope that his bullet would find its mark. And at last I knew he was ahead, and could begin to breathe again.

Almost immediately on the heels of the shot I thought I heard a shout behind me. But I couldn't stop. I couldn't let Dell get away. I couldn't let him reach the beginning of the circle I'd made or the pursued would become the pursuer and I would find him behind me again.

I speeded up, running now with a kind of breathless desperation. Past me, no more than twenty feet away, thundered half a dozen horsemen. I yelled, but they missed seeing me.

The horsemen could be none other than Pa and the K Diamond crew. They must have despaired of doing anything for the cattle in such a storm, and turned back toward home. They must have heard Dell's shot as they rode into the yard, and had come to investigate.

Probably they thought they were riding to the aid of someone lost in the snow, a mistaken idea that wouldn't be dispelled until Dell's first bullet blasted one of them from his saddle. And that one might well be Pa.

I screamed into the howling wind, "Pa! It's Dell! Look out!" but my voice was snatched from my lips and hurled impotently downward.

Before me I heard another shot, louder than the first, because it was pointed toward me instead of away from me.

In my mind I could see the startled surprise written on Pa's face. I could see it change to pain, could see him beginning to fall. I ran faster, harder.

I kept waiting, waiting for what I knew must come. It

was slow in coming because of the storm, because of cold, gloved hands, of awkward sheepskin coats. But come it did, a flurry of shots that sounded like so many firecrackers.

That would be the volley that riddled Dell Anson.

As suddenly as though I had plunged around a turn, I came upon them, a group of rearing, frightened horses, of shouting men. My eyes searched for Pa, and the held breath ran out of me with intense relief as I saw him, tall and ponderous in his saddle.

On the ground was a still, crumpled form, and blood stained the snow bright scarlet beside him.

Ches was down, nudging the still form with the toe of his boot.

He turned as I skidded to a halt beside him. He yelled up at Pa, "He's dead."

I looked at Pa, noticing for the first time that one of his arms dangled straight down from his body, swinging like a limp rag with the movement of his horse. His face was gray, and contorted with pain. Blood dripped from the bare fingers of his hand as steadily as rain from the eaves of a house during a summer shower.

Pa spoke from between clenched teeth, "Bring his body in with you." Then he seemed to notice me for the first time. "What are you doing here?"

"Dell jumped me in the barn." It was important to me suddenly that Pa understood what had happened, and my part in it. "I didn't want to kill him. So I led him out away from the barn. Then I circled and came up behind him. I was tracking him when you rode past me." I realized that

187

I was shouting, and I knew I wanted not only Pa to understand, but the crew as well.

Ches noticed my ear and leaned closer to look. "A bullet?" he shouted.

I nodded. "Back there in the barn." The ear was growing painful now. It burned and throbbed and sent shooting pains clear through my head.

Ches jerked his head toward the house. Then, leading his horse, he moved away after Pa and the others toward it. A couple of crewmen lingered long enough to load Dell's body.

At the barn, they dismounted, and Pa and Ches and I went on toward the house. Pa was staggering now, and I took hold of his good arm to steady him. He flung off my hand with a gesture of impatience, and the exertion almost made him fall.

Left alone, he'd crawl away somewhere to lick his wounds like a wolf, sick and near to death but asking help from no one. But he'd meet his match in Dolly, I knew, in the clean clothes and hot water and healing salves she'd use on him.

We staggered into the house, the pair of us dripping blood, and slumped down together into the horsehair sofa before the fire. Dolly glanced from Pa to me and back again, and then she ran from the room on light, hurrying feet and I heard her call to Franklin for hot water and heard drawers slamming in the kitchen as she hunted bandages and disinfectants and a surgeon's probe to remove the bullet.

Rose stood with her back to the fire looking at us, her

eyes wide, her face almost as gray as Pa's. Her lips formed the word, "Dell?" and I said reluctantly, "He's dead, Rose. The crew shot him down after he wounded Pa."

Her breath sighed out, as though she had been holding it. An expression of stark relief touched her face and was gone. Then she was down on her knees, snatching clean white cloths from Dolly and mopping at my bleeding ear with them.

Her relief was not because Dell was dead, I knew, but because I had not killed him.

Her hands were gentle, almost fearful as they cleaned my ear and bandaged it. There was softness and tenderness in her eyes that I had never seen there before. It was as though she could not bear to hurt me.

I was realizing for the first time the complexities that went into a man's love for a woman. So many things besides the physical desire to possess her. So many things, all mixed up together, but dovetailing until each was inseparable from the other. I knew as she knelt there before me that I would love her as long as I lived.

This must have been the way Pa loved my mother, and I could begin to understand the wrath and fury that consumed him the night she died. I could begin to understand the burning need to destroy that had overpowered him until he had no thought but that.

I looked at Pa, who was near to fainting with pain as Ches probed his upper arm for the bullet. Then I looked at Dolly, who stood clinging to the mantel, her heart in her eyes as she looked at my father.

And yet nothing was changed between them. As implacable as ever, he would move against Owens and his family as soon as the storm cleared. And Dolly would leave.

We had all taken our stands for what we believed in to be right. Dell had died already, but that wasn't the end. The hand must be played out to the last card until death's bony fingers raked the chips from the top of the table.

The days passed thereafter with a sort of tense, waiting monotony, and all the while, night and day, the wind screamed at the house. Snow rattled against the windows until it piled high against them and deadened the sound of the beating wings of wind.

Cattle drifted through the yard occasionally, dumb and plodding. They drifted and died, and the gulches filled with their bodies until those that came later could cross the frozen carcasses of their predecessors. They died standing up, some of them, legs spraddled to brace themselves against the wind, died and froze solid standing until a man had to ride close to know they had crossed the line between life and death.

We no longer saw K Diamond cattle, but instead saw cattle bearing the brands of outfits as far north as Wyoming. Like tumbleweeds driven before a spring wind, they piled against every obstacle, died where they stopped, and froze where they died.

With each successive day, a little more of the life went out of my father, and a little more death seeped into his gaunt face, and emptied his hollow eyes.

A bunch of riders came into the yard, near dead from exposure, all of them, carrying the frozen bodies of three of their comrades. They'd tried to drift with their cattle, in the hope of saving a few, of driving the remainder back when the fury of the storm had spent itself. Beaten, they stayed at K Diamond, and Dolly and Rose made many trips to the bunkhouse to treat their frost-bitten extremities.

Ches and Pa were bitter-eyed strangers, glaring at each other whenever their paths crossed, which was often, for Ches would not allow Dolly to minister to anyone unless he was beside her to help. He carried her load of water, or food, or bandages. He'd muffle a hurt man's mouth with his hand to silence the curse that pain made it impossible to repress. And all the while his eyes were as devoted, as undemanding as a faithful dog's.

Rose, dressed in Dolly's clothes, which were small for her and which therefore made me painfully conscious of her lovely body, avoided me as much as possible. At first I was hurt by her avoidance, but one day I surprised the reason for it in her eyes—her want, her need, her guilt because her husband was so recently dead.

The crew had made him a coffin and it lay in the lean-to behind the bunkhouse along with three others containing the frozen punchers and a fourth containing a man who had since died of frostbite. The dead waited, as did everything else, for an end to the terrible, killing blizzard. . . .

All things have their ending, and so did the blizzard.

I will never forget waking one day half an hour before

dawn with a puzzled, frightened wonder at whatever it was that had wakened me.

For several minutes I lay motionless in my bed, aware of a deep, crawling uneasiness. And at last I placed it. It was not noise which had awakened me but rather the complete lack of it.

I bounced out of my bed and ran to the window. I scrubbed for several moments at the caked frost on its pane before I had a hole large enough to look through. Then I saw the stars, bright as a million lanterns in the sky, and I became aware that the wind had stopped. Like a tomb the earth lay stretching away toward the horizon. The snow had stopped falling; the air was clear.

My hands trembled as I pulled on my clothes. Carrying my boots, I ran out into the living room.

Franklin was building a fire in the fireplace. Pa was standing at the window, looking out through a hole he had scraped in the frost. He had more strength today than at any time since he'd been shot. The listlessness was gone from his eyes; his face was flushed with color. Waiting had been hard for him, but now the waiting was over.

Dolly came running in, her face as excited as a child's. Rose followed her, calling, "Jeff! Oh, Jeff, it's over. The storm's stopped."

She drew me over to a window, and together we scraped a hole in the frost and looked through, our heads touching. In the east, dawn fingered the horizon, tracing it with a deep gray that lightened gradually until it was pink.

She whispered, "Jeff, I can't go back. I can't go back to the badlands."

My voice was shaking. "Then come away with me."

She looked up at me, a naked longing in her eyes, a kind of dazed unbelief. "Now? This morning?"

I wanted to nod, to tell her yes, that we'd go today. But I had to shake my head. Going away with Rose would have to wait on Pa, on whatever he intended doing about the Owens family. I knew that if I went now, I would be betraying something within myself. I would be dodging an issue that had to be faced.

I said softly, "No. Not today. It will have to wait for a little while, Rose."

She knew. And I believe she understood me, possibly better than I did myself. Yet something went out of her eyes, something good, and in its place was born a stark kind of fear.

We turned around and went toward the breakfast table in the dining room, and I realized suddenly that we must have been at the window a lot longer than either of us had intended.

Dolly was watching Pa at the head of the table. There was a question in Dolly's eyes, a fearful hope.

Ches came in from outside and sat down beside me. The sun came up and sent its bright shafts of light through the holes we'd scrubbed in the frosted window-panes. It put a warm glow upon the whole room, as though the world had wakened from its deathlike sleep, and today would begin again to live.

The sun should have cheered us all, yet its effect was

the exact opposite. I realized that we were all watching Pa, that in all our minds was the thought, "What about Owens? What are you going to do?"

As though he had been asked the question directly, he said suddenly and harshly, "Nothing's changed. Nothing at all. Today we'll start in where we left off the day the storm started."

The faint hope that had lived in Dolly's eyes now died. Ches cleared his throat and said, "I'll draw my time this morning, Rob. I'm leaving today."

Pa didn't even acknowledge his words. He only gave Ches a sour, contemptuous stare. He looked at Dolly afterward, a question in his eyes. She murmured, meeting his glance, "You said it, Rob, I didn't. Nothing's changed. Nothing's different."

So it was to be Pa and me at the end.

Was this, I wondered, what we had lived for and worked toward all these years? Was this inevitable conflict to be the end of everything? There could be no winner today, I knew. Only losers.

In dead silence we finished breakfast. Ches left to pack, and as he went out, Pa said harshly, "Tell the crew to get ready. We're moving Owens first thing this morning."

Ches nodded silently, and Dolly began to cry. I went to my room to get my coat, and I strapped the old Dance Brothers and Park revolver on outside my coat.

As I turned to go, I almost collided with Rose, standing in the door of my room. "Why is he this way, Jeff?"

I shrugged bitterly. "I don't know. But it's the way he is."

"What will you do? What can you do?"

"Whatever has to be done, I suppose."

"You mean you'd kill your own father?"

My face twisted. "Rose, don't make it any harder than it already is."

"All right, Jeff. But when you come back you'll find me waiting."

Her eyes were bright with unshed tears. Her eyes did the begging her lips refused to do. In all honesty I'll have to admit I wavered, too. It would be so damned much easier to turn my back on what I knew was right—so much easier just to take Rose and go away.

I suppose only my fear made it possible for me to hold onto my resolution. Fear that when the showdown came I would measure up no better than I ever had. But I had to know. I had to know if I would back down forever before the implacable giant who was my father.

The endless preparations were a nightmare, but at last we rode out in the blinding sunlight, and plunged our horses through the deep drifts as we headed southward.

The air was sterile, cold and still. I don't believe Pa realized to quite what extent the storm had taken its toll. But as we rode, I could see it coming over him.

We saw no single live thing in all this gleaming waste—no cattle, no horses, no wild thing save for the gray and hungry wolves we'd find tearing at some frozen carcass at the edge of a pile of frozen carcasses.

Even with the visual evidence before his own eyes, I believe we were nearly to the Owens place before the full knowledge hit Pa that K Diamond was wiped out. Its thousands of cattle had suffered the same fate as those we saw, except that most of them had reached some range farther south before it caught up with them.

His face was terrible. All of these long years he had fought to build, fought to hold, until it had become his obsession. He had clung to his own before every threat his fellow man could throw against him. And now, in the last week, he had lost everything. What remained was only a homestead claim on K Diamond's buildings, a few scattered homestead claims on a few scattered water holes. The rest was gone.

And of those he loved, none were left. Dolly was lost. Ches would be leaving, for I knew he'd be unwilling to stay in the face of Pa's unjust accusation of him. I would be leaving with Rose.

A lesser man would have broken before such a combination of blows. Pa didn't, even though his broad, mighty shoulders slumped with desperation, even though a dead emptiness came to his eyes.

I couldn't credit the feeling I had that he really felt no enthusiasm for this, but was only going through with it because of his implacable stubbornness.

Yet for Pa, there remained one more blow, and I steeled myself to administer it as we rode into sight of the last low rise that stood between us and the Owens homestead.

I spurred my horse ahead, passed him and stopped, turning. I said in a voice so strong it surprised me, "Pa, this is far enough."

He knew what I meant—it needed no explanation. I could see that he had been waiting for it.

My forlorn hope that he would change, that he would turn back, was gone now. Now remained only the bitter ashes of what had once been between us as father and son.

His great head came up, and his eyes once again flashed. His great, tawny mustache was hoary with the frost of his heavy breathing.

I was ready to die, and knew I would, yet there was no longer any fear in me. I could meet his eyes with my own.

I'd never been a very religious person, and the insides of churches were strange to me. Yet each man has his own inner beliefs, and from these came my feeling that something greater than any of us had done this. Pa had set himself up as God. He'd played the part through, faithfully, but he'd reached the end of the string. Something had intervened, had demonstrated with a single blow how puny is man and man's creations.

The crew bunched and moved away uneasily, awed by the sight of father and son tensed over their guns and ready to kill.

Seconds became hours as our glances met and held. The world stood still and the silence was like a blanket, covering and smothering us.

Even the horses were still, as though held motionless by something beyond their control or ability to understand. Pa's hand moved slowly, terribly, inexorably toward the grip of his gun.

A spark of insane fury was born in the back of his eyes. It leaped and grew as the flames of a grass fire grow, and it poured over me in a virulent flood that turned every fiber of me cold.

And yet, within me, was not even the desire to stand aside. As though all of my life had pointed to this moment, I knew I could not have dropped my glance from his if I had wanted to. I knew, in that instant, that if the strength were needed to draw my gun and fire against him, I would find it. It would be inside me when the need for it came.

Then, as though the fuel which fed it were gone, the flame of fury behind his eyes began to die. It is, perhaps, the strangest, most elusive thing in my memory, but I knew it, though there was no visible change in his expression.

He didn't break. He didn't even seem to retreat. Yet the change was there and I remembered the odd reluctance I'd sensed in him earlier today.

One instant we were facing each other like a pair of snarling wolves, and the next all danger was gone. I sensed it, the crew sensed it, and even the horses felt it for they began to fidget and move around as though even they were aware that the tension and danger had magically gone from the air.

His arm dropped limply to his side but he lost no stature as he said almost inaudibly, "You're right, of course. I've known it all along. But until just now I wouldn't admit it even to myself. Ride on in to the Owens place by yourself, Jeff, and see if they're all right. Tell them I'll raise no hand against them."

I couldn't keep the tears of pure relief from flooding

my eyes. So that the crew wouldn't see, I turned away and plunged my horse over the rise toward the Owens shack.

It was leveled to the ground, blown down by the wind. But out of the dinky spud cellar they had dug now poured the Owens family, all of them, stamping and flinging their arms around to warm their stiff, chilled bodies. Dave Owens, seeing me, shambled back into the cellar and when he came out, he carried a rifle.

They looked at me out of dulled, apathetic eyes, aware that they were beaten, that no fight was possible now. I said, "Keep yourselves going until nightfall. I'll send a wagonload of supplies to you from K Diamond."

Uncomprehending and unbelieving, they stared at me. I said, "You're all right now. You can stay. There'll be no trouble, now or ever again."

Still they did not seem to understand, but I knew they would in time, when the shock of all this had passed.

I turned my horse and rode back toward the place where Pa and the crew were waiting. I saw him as I came over the rise, sitting a little apart from the crew. His great head was raised, and he sat taller in the saddle than he ever had before.

The hot blue flame was back in his eyes and he was just as implacable as he had ever been. I knew that K Diamond would rise again from its own ashes, that new herds would spring from the bleaching bones of the old.

He wasn't changed. No man can change entirely in a few moments' time. But I felt a gradual change had begun in Pa as it had in the country itself. The old days were gone. Law would come and both Pa and the wild country would gradually be forced to accept it.

For the first time in my life I knew there was a place for me here rebuilding K Diamond—and more important, rebuilding the things that had once been between us as father and son. I knew I'd stay. We'd differ again, perhaps many times. But now, each difference would be easier of solution because in us both would be the memory of this day.

No words were spoken between us. But with the crew at our backs, we turned and rode toward home, toward the two women who awaited us, so certain that only one of us would come riding in.

No longer could the day's sterile cold stay the warmth that flooded my body. I looked at Pa and grinned, and today he grinned right back.

Center Point Publishing
600 Brooks Road ● PO Box 1
Thorndike ME 04986-0001 USA

(207) 568-3717

US & Canada:
1 800 929-9108